The Impostor:
Half a Hero

by Richard Lee Byers

THE IMPOSTOR: HALF A HERO

by Richard Lee Byers

Rothco Press • Los Angeles, California

Published by
Rothco Press
8033 West Sunset Blvd., Ste. 1022
West Hollywood, CA 90046

Cover design by Rob Cohen

Rothco Press is a division of Over Easy Media Inc.

ISBN: 978-1-941519-91-2

Electronic ISBN: 978-1-941519-92-9

Also by Richard Lee Byers

Deathward

Fright Line

The Vampire's Apprentice

Dark Fortune

Dead Time

Joy Ride

Warlock Games

Party Till You Drop

The Tale of the Terrible Toys

Soul Killer

Caravan of Shadows

The Ebon Mask

Dark Kingdoms (includes The Ebon Mask and completes the story that novel began)

Netherworld

On A Darkling Plain

Forsaken

Forsworn

Forbidden

The Enemy Within

The Q Word and Other Stories

Zombies in Paradise

The Shattered Mask

Queen of the Depths

The Black Bouquet

Dissolution

The Rage

The Rite

The Ruin

Year of Rogue Dragons (collects The Rage, The Rite, and The Ruin plus two bonus stories)

Unclean

Undead

Unholy

The Captive Flame

Whisper of Venom

The Spectral Blaze

The Masked Witches

Prophet of the Dead

Called to Darkness

Blind God's Bluff

The Reaver

The Impostor #1: Half a Hero

Black Dogs

The Impostor #2: The Blood Machine (forthcoming)

This Sword for Hire (forthcoming)

Black Crowns (forthcoming)

Suiting Up

Matt Brown was walking home through Germantown after an evening workout at the gym, craving a beer and wondering if he needed to write up Eddie for coming in late and sneaking out early. He hoped not. He'd try talking to the guy one more time.

Then he noticed the other people on the street, who were likely walking either to the Kaiser Street bars and clubs to the north, the municipal parking garage to the south, or apartments and condos here in the neighborhood. Many had their phones out, either pressed to their ears or held in front of them, the screens glowing in the gloom. Their voices sounded tense, agitated, or both.

Frowning, Matt wondered if something important–a natural disaster, maybe—was going on somewhere, and if he should ask one of his fellow pedestrians or dig out his own phone and check the news for himself. Then, in the distance, something boomed. The sidewalk shuddered beneath him, and the windows of boutiques, galleries, and restaurants rattled. People cried out, and car alarms started blaring.

Matt looked around but couldn't see what had exploded. The old brownstones lining the narrow street cut off his view. Instead, he spotted something worse.

Shapes came flying out of the north. It was hard to make them out in the dark, especially since they were moving so fast, but they reminded him of insects. Maybe it was the buzzing noise they made.

Some of the shapes swooped lower. Blue rays stabbed down, striking two of the people on the street. Matt couldn't tell exactly what the beams did to them, but they both collapsed. Elsewhere, more explosions boomed.

For a second, the situation felt dreamlike. Unreal. Naturally, he understood that a thing like this *could* happen. But it never did. Not to him.

It was, though, and he and all these other people had to get under cover. As more blue beams flickered, and his fellow pedestrians screamed, he scurried to the door to a vintage clothing shop. It was locked. So was the entry to the music store beside it.

It occurred to him that Kaiser Street was just a block away, and every one of the dozens of bars was open at eleven o'clock at night. He was going to die because he hadn't given in to that hankering for a beer.

Then a man pointed upward and shouted, "Red Bear!" Others took up the cry, their voices now charged with hope.

Red Bear stood on a rooftop, where the lights intended to illuminate the insurance-company advertisement painted on a water tower also revealed his massive frame. Matt had never before seen him, or any superhero, in person but recognized him from all the photos and video. Dressed in russet fur and brown leather, Red Bear looked like a Viking in a movie. His huge arms were bare except for wristbands studded with claws.

Matt was as happy to see Red Bear as everyone else, but even so, he wondered how the huge man could cope with the menaces darting and hovering over the street. Like his teammate Magnetar, Red Bear was considered one of Jackson City's two most powerful heroes, but unlike Magnetar, he couldn't fly.

Red Bear solved that problem by stooping and ripping a chunk of stone from a cornice. He threw it, and it crashed into one of the larger flying shapes. The thing plummeted and smashed down in the street. The glow of a nearby streetlight revealed it was a machine, an airship or robot, but Matt's initial impression had been correct: It did look like an insect. The body had a segmented, tripartite structure, and both the outstretched wings and the two round, bulging masses at the front were made of crystal.

Red Bear tore loose another piece of stone. When blue rays streaked at him, he used it as a shield, and then, once the barrage let up, he hurled that one, too. It slammed into a smaller airborne shape, with a thump rather than a crash, and traveled onward with its target stuck to the front of it like a bug on a windshield. They banged down a street or two over, where Matt couldn't see.

So far, Red Bear was doing so well that Matt wondered if the flyers might break off the attack. But instead, they circled so they could shoot at the hero from all sides, and after that, even though he was quick, especially for such a big man, he couldn't dodge or shield himself from every ray. The energy didn't knock him down like it had the ordinary people in the street, but he jerked and stiffened when it hit.

Apparently, that was encouraging enough to make the flying things decide they wouldn't need all their strength to defeat him. Several turned away and reoriented on the people in the street.

Most of whom had paused to watch their champion defend them. But now, once again, they shrieked and bolted, Matt sprinting along with the rest. He wondered how many doors he could try before a ray zapped him.

But then, up ahead, a door opened all by itself. Well, no, not really. But the figure inside was so difficult to spot in the gloom that for a moment, Matt hadn't been able to make him out.

Even now, it was hard to discern detail, but the man seemed to be wearing a gray-black outer garment that reminded Matt of Sherlock Holmes, a long coat with a waist-length cape attachment in place of sleeves. A dark, close-fitting mask covered his head, and the broad brim of his hat obscured his face even more if that was possible.

He was the vigilante known as Dr. Umbra. Matt had heard that he customarily spoke in an eerie whisper, but he bellowed when he called, "This way!" Matt dashed toward the promise of safety.

He passed Dr. Umbra stalking in the opposite direction. Even up close, the superhero looked murky and blurry like a ghost. He didn't acknowledge Matt. His attention was on the fly-ers. He flexed the fingers of his black-gloved hands and suddenly held a pistol in each.

Matt reached the entrance. On the other side was a vestibule ringed with doors leading to medical offices of one sort or an-other. Dr. Umbra had opened one of them, no doubt so people could hide in the rooms beyond.

That was exactly what Matt wanted to do. But despite the fear howling through his mind, he realized he was the *only* person to arrive at the entrance. He looked back to see what had become of everyone else.

Some people were running in his direction. He'd simply got-ten to the doorway ahead of them. But others were rushing on by, and he realized it was no wonder. With the explosions now booming nonstop and all the other noise, they hadn't heard Dr. Umbra shout, nor, with so much else going on, had they noticed where he'd come from.

Somebody needed to attract their attention. Matt stayed out-side the door, waved his arms, and yelled as loud as he could. "Over here! Over here!"

Dr. Umbra positioned himself in the middle of the street and started shooting upward. Pulses of shadow, almost impossi-ble to see in the night but somehow even darker, flickered from the muzzles of his pistols.

The flying things returned fire. His caped coat swirling about him, Dr. Umbra simply dodged the first rays. Then, as more beams flashed down, he started vanishing for a second or half second at a time, then reappearing in a different spot.

But finally he stopped flickering in and out of view and stood still, like he needed to catch his breath or didn't know what to do next. Several blue rays stabbed down all at once and hit him.

Matt winced, then realized the beams had passed right through the vigilante's body to splash against the brick pavement. Seemingly unharmed, Dr. Umbra sidestepped and resumed fir-ing. Two of the smaller flyers slammed down in the street.

And as the fight raged on, Matt yelled himself hoarse. Some people ran on by even so, but he pulled in most of them. Until there was nobody left in the street but the people the rays had found and Dr. Umbra.

The hero whirled, sprinted toward the doorway, and nearly reached it before a ray hit him in the back. This time, the attack didn't pass right on through his body. He dropped to one knee.

But he was just a stride away. Matt could grab him and haul him inside. He lunged to do so.

Dark shapes swooped lower. He saw a blue flickering and just had time to decide he was going to die before everything went black.

He knew he *hadn't* died when he woke with a gasp. His heart pounding, he looked around.

Or at least he tried. It was dark, with just a few streaks of dimly glowing red on the ceiling providing light, and, making things even murkier, an essentially transparent but tinted and curved cover separated him from everything he was straining to see.

It was obvious, though, that he lay on a sort of domed rect-angular table—or pedestal—in a room full of them. Everything had a smooth, flowing look to it, like the makers had shaped it out of clay or blown it out of molten glass.

It could only mean the flying things had taken him prisoner, and with that realization came a fresh jolt of fear. It suddenly felt like there was no air under the cover, and he reached up to shove at it.

As soon as he touched it, it split down the middle. The two halves melted into jelly, which then drained down into the edges of the pedestal. Or at least he thought they did. It happened so fast, he wasn't certain of the details.

Nor did he care. All that mattered was that he could get up. He started to, then felt a tug at the back of his head.

Investigating by touch, he found he was wearing a ring of metal like a crown without the points, and that a short cable connected it to the top of the pedestal. He suspected it was this and not the cover that was supposed to hold him in place, and that it worked by keeping a prisoner unconscious. Fortunately, it had quit doing that.

He pulled it off, then started to sit up once again. Something boomed like a thunderclap, and the room shook. He froze.

A part of him wanted to *stay* frozen, too. It had had too much of explosions and danger and simply wanted to cower.

But that would be stupid. He didn't understand much of what was happening, but it was clear luck had given him a chance to escape. If he threw it away, he was unlikely to get another.

He struggled to stop panting and breathe slowly and deeply. Once he managed that, he swung his legs over the side of the pedestal and stood up.

He took another look around. All the other pedestals were empty. An arch opened on a corridor.

An even louder bang shook everything. Staggering, he snatched the edge of the platform from which he'd just risen to keep from falling down.

He seemed to be in some kind of enemy fortress, and maybe it was banging and shaking because the good guys were attacking it. Maybe he *should* sit tight and wait for the Army or superheroes to burst in and rescue him.

Or maybe not. There wouldn't be a rescue if the attack failed, or if it brought the whole place crashing down on top of him.

Matt realized he had no way of knowing what was really the smart thing to do. He simply had to follow his instincts, and they said that trying to help himself was preferable to just sitting back down and waiting for something to happen.

He tiptoed to the arch, peered, and listened. As far as he could tell, the passage ahead was empty. He prowled on, past a section of wall seeping slime, a row of holes at knee level, and a hexagonal screen full of angular yellow symbols he'd never seen before.

Another boom, another bone-shaking bump, and something buzzed. The sound came from an arch just ahead on the left.

Matt scrambled through the nearest opening on the right. That put him out of sight of anyone or anything that might step out into the corridor, and now, he suspected, he should stay absolutely still until the buzzing went away.

But scared as he was, he was also curious to know who or what had attacked the city, and it was even possible the knowledge could save his life. His mouth dry, he peeked back out into the passage.

At a pair of wasps, each as big as a Great Dane.

Except no. Not *quite* wasps. They had the round black eyes, hanging antennae, and jagged mandibles. The double pairs of clear, shivering wings, and the striped abdomen tapering to a sting. But the stripes were red and black, not yellow and black, and a pair of segmented arms grew between the head and the first pair of legs. Those forelimbs ended in complicated tangles of finger- and pincer-like extremities.

The creatures were fascinating and horrifying. They made Matt want to stare and cringe at the same time. He went with the latter, jerking back before the insects noticed him.

It's an alien invasion, he thought, his heart pounding, *not just a supervillain or a terrorist organization like AURA making trouble.* He'd already suspected as much, but now he knew for sure.

He tried to match what he'd just seen to old news footage about extraterrestrial visitors and races. He couldn't, although that didn't necessarily mean anything. He'd never cared enough about such things to pay much attention. They hadn't seemed to have anything to do with him.

He wished that were still the case.

He waited until the buzzing receded and fell silent, then peeked back out into the corridor. The wasp-things were gone. Scared that he would accidentally catch up with them, or blunder into the view of other creatures just like them, he nevertheless crept onward.

Other passages ran away to the right and left, and he won-dered if he'd do better to head down one of those. It was entirely possible, but once again, he had no way of knowing, and as long as he kept heading in a straight line, he'd at least know where he was in relation to the room in which he'd awakened. Not that he wanted to go back there, but it was the only reference point he had.

Another boom and jolt knocked chips out of the ceiling. Some were bits of the glowing red streaks, which kept on shining after they broke loose.

Matt peered through another arch. He caught his breath.

This room contained pedestals, too. But they were coverless and there were only four, which left more space to move around among them. Corpses lay on the two slabs nearer to the doors. Each was naked, split and spread open from throat to crotch, the top of the skull removed to expose the brain. Tools dangled from the ceiling over the bodies, and more of the yellow symbols glowed on the hexagonal screens on the walls.

The aliens were dissecting the poor bastards. His stomach churning, Matt started to turn away, then noticed the articles on the pedestals by the far wall.

One surface held garments of fur and leather. On the other sat a pair of pistols, gloves, a mask, a cloak, and a broad-brimmed hat, all the items murky and indistinct, like shadows.

Matt's nausea gave way to a more complex tangle of emo-tion, grief, anger, and dismay all knotted together. Red Bear and Dr. Umbra had died fighting to protect him and the other strang-ers in the street. They deserved a lot better than being cut apart like lab rats.

Unfortunately, it seemed doubtful that anyone would ever be able to punish the aliens for their disrespect. If even superheroes hadn't been able to beat them, who could? More to the point, what real hope did Matt have of even making it out of their fortress in one piece?

Quite possibly none. But then he realized something about the corpses.

They looked...ordinary.

Both men had been fit, muscular, but they didn't appear much more so than the average gym rat like Matt himself. Red Bear had shrunk from eight feet tall to the height of a normal man and dropped hundreds of pounds in the process. Dr. Umbra didn't look shadowy and insubstantial anymore. Only his outfit did.

What if, instead of something innate, the source of the heroes' powers had resided in their costumes or equipment? Matt had heard of such things, gadgets and allegedly mystical talismans that transformed the user. If that was the way it had been, could he use the same articles to escape?

As he hurried across the room, another boom and shock staggered him. He almost fell on top of the pedestal holding Red Bear's body, but caught his balance in time. He reached the heroes' effects, then hesitated, suddenly unsure if it was right to take them.

Scowling, he brushed his qualms aside. Red Bear and Dr. Umbra wouldn't want the aliens to keep possession of their stuff, would they? They'd want Matt to steal it back to save himself as they'd been trying to save him, then turn it over to...well, whoever should get it. He'd figure that part out later.

It was easy to decide which hero's stuff to check out first. Red Bear's powers had been awesome for fighting, but that was the last thing Matt wanted to do. He simply wanted to get away, and it was Dr. Umbra who'd been famous for his ability to sneak around.

He picked up the hat and cloak and got a surprise. There was nothing special about the T-shirt, sweatpants, and Nikes underneath. Apparently, wrapped in shadow and blur, Dr. Umbra hadn't needed a complete superhero costume to look impressive.

Well, good. That simplified things a little.

Another boom and shock made Matt flinch. It made him want to get a move on, too.

He examined the long coat. It was surprisingly lightweight, made of a fabric he couldn't identify, and had holsters on the inside to hold the pistols. He slipped them in, then pulled on the garment.

For a moment, it was tight in the shoulders. Then, startling a gasp out of him, it squirmed and refitted itself to his frame.

But nothing else happened. He still felt like himself. Ordinary.

He put on the black gloves, then flexed his fingers like Dr. Umbra had. The pistols did *not* appear in his hands. He could feel that they were still riding below his armpits like before.

Sighing, he decided that maybe he'd been wrong. Maybe Dr. Umbra's powers had been innate, or mostly so. Still, guns were guns, and camouflage was camouflage. He pulled on the vigilante's mask.

A bolt of pain stabbed down the length of his body. He fell down and writhed. He couldn't tell what was happening to him, a heart attack, seizure, or what, but it was bad. Maybe even bad enough to kill him.

He raised his hand to his head and fumbled at the close-fitting mask, trying to pull it off. He couldn't get hold of it. The pain was so excruciating that it robbed him of the requisite motor control.

Then he heard a dry, dispassionate voice: "The level of pain will decrease for sixty seconds. During that interval, you will divest yourself of the equipment and return it to its rightful owner."

"Please," Matt gritted, "listen to me."

"Emergency protocols are in effect," the voice continued. "If you are still in possession of the equipment when the sixty seconds run out, you will die."

"You don't understand! Dr. Umbra is dead! The aliens killed him! I need his stuff to escape from them!"

There was a pause, and then the voice said, "Assessing." A moment after that, the pain stopped as suddenly as it had started.

Trembling, Matt clambered to his feet. "Hello?" he said, and got another surprise. His voice was now a creepy whisper that belonged in a horror movie.

Then the room brightened. Scared that the aliens had come in and turned on additional lights, he jerked around.

Nothing was there. He belatedly realized the ambient light hadn't changed; he was better able to see because the mask had given him night vision, just as it was altering his voice.

He'd been right. The costume *had* been the source of many if not all of Dr. Umbra's abilities, and now they were coming online.

"Hello?" he repeated. "Did you switch on the costume for me? *Are* you the costume?"

The voice didn't answer. For whatever reason, Matt was on his own again.

On his own, but maybe a lot better off than he'd been before. He flexed his fingers.

The pistols still wouldn't jump. But something else happened. He suddenly sensed his equipment was fully charged. It was like he had a gauge inside his head.

If he had a full tank of gas, he should be able to disappear like Dr. Umbra had on the street. He willed it to happen and watched his hands and forearms fade away.

For the first time since the aliens had appeared, he felt a little bit safe, and that was why he was reluctant to make himself reappear. But he suspected invisibility was one of the functions that used energy. Otherwise, Dr. Umbra would have stayed that way all the time. So Matt should save it for when he really needed it.

The hero's other power had been to turn insubstantial like a ghost. Matt tried to will himself into that condition and then to stick his fingertips into the pedestal, but to no avail. Despite his shadowy appearance, he was as solid as ever.

He put on the broad-brimmed hat, and it too wriggled, adjusting the fit. Then he turned to Red Bear's effects.

He didn't like the thought of leaving the giant's costume behind to serve as the wasp-things' trophy. He *definitely* didn't want to leave them the source of Red Bear's powers if, in fact, it was here. But he doubted he could sneak out of the fortress carrying all this bulky fur and leather. So he went through it looking for anything that seemed both portable and important and in due course picked up one of the claw-studded wristbands.

Despite the need for quiet, he almost cried out. Somehow, just touching the claw-studded leather filled him with wonder and awe, like looking at pictures from the Hubble telescope or gazing out across the Grand Canyon. But it was also scary, like he was was teetering on the very edge of the canyon fighting a crazy urge to jump.

Magic, he thought. There really was such a thing, and this was what it felt like: too dangerous to mess around with, but also too powerful to leave for the wasps. He stuffed the wristbands into one of the caped coat's pockets.

Last, he drew one of the pistols and looked it over. The weapon differed considerably from the firearms he and his team sold at his sporting-goods store. There was no muzzle at the end of the barrel, nor, as far as he could tell, any safety or way to reload. He supposed it was a raygun, a supergun, and thus as strange to him as the rest of Dr. Umbra's gear. He just had to hope that if he pointed it and pulled the trigger, it would do what he needed it to.

Or rather, to hope he wouldn't need it to do anything.

He guessed he was ready. He crept to the arch, and peeked out into the corridor. It was empty, so, pistol still in hand, he skulked onward.

Another boom and shock knocked loose bigger pieces of the ceiling, exposing and breaking tubes snaking through a fibrous substance that looked like flesh. A gray fluid that smelled like burning plastic spurted down from the breached pipes or veins.

The spray filled the passage from one wall to the other. Wondering if the stuff was toxic, he hesitated, then heard more buzzing, loud and plainly close at hand.

For an instant, a stab of fear robbed him of the ability to think, and then he remembered Dr. Umbra's abilities. He willed himself invisible, and what he could see of himself vanished as it had before.

Just in time. Three wasps scuttled out of an arch, up the wall, and onto the ceiling, where, clinging, they began to stop the leakage by puking up a white paste and spreading it like plaster.

Unfortunately, it was taking a while, and Matt doubted it was a good idea to just stand motionless and wait for them to finish. For all he knew, they might eventually smell him or detect him some other way, or he might run out of juice to power his invisibility.

He took a breath, preparing himself to tiptoe right underneath them, and then realized how the spray would reveal his shape. Intent on their work, the insects might not notice, but did he want to bet his life on it?

Not so you'd notice it. It was time to check out one of the branching passages he'd passed by before. Finger on the trigger of the pistol, he crept back the way he'd come.

And made it through an arch without the aliens ever sensing him. He checked his internal meter and perceived that Dr. Umbra's equipment still had most of its charge.

He grinned because all this showed he really did have a chance. If he could only find an exit, he could slip past any sentries and escape.

He made himself visible and prowled onward, looking through one opening after another. Until he came to a room like the one in which he'd awakened, except that this one had a prisoner on each of the two dozen slabs.

It chilled Matt to realize just how lucky he'd been. The wasps had apparently filled up this room first, and he'd been the one captive leftover. So they'd stuck him in a second cell, where the pounding the fort was taking interrupted the flow of power to his sleep-inducing headgear. If there'd been one less prisoner, or if the insects had randomly chosen someone else to put in the second room, Matt would still be lying helpless.

As these people were. What was he going to do about it?

He *wanted* to help them. But Dr. Umbra's costume couldn't make them all sneaky. The sad truth was, it couldn't hide anybody but the wearer, and that meant Matt could only save himself. If he tried to do more, he'd just be throwing his life away for nothing.

After I get out, he silently promised, *I'll tell the authorities you're here. That's all I can do.*

But despite that entirely sensible decision, he found he couldn't make himself move on.

Maybe it was because he *had* been so lucky. Lucky to wake up. Lucky to find the superheroes' equipment. Lucky the mysterious voice hadn't exploded his brain or whatever it had planned to do. He obviously didn't deserve that kind of good fortune any more than any of these others, and somehow, that would make abandoning them feel like an unbearably selfish, gutless thing to do.

The selfish, gutless part of him wishing he'd never stumbled across them, he hurried into the cell.

In the second row, he found a big-boned forty-something woman in a pale green uniform with a nametag that read Sally Hollingsworth, RN. Sally had a strong, intelligent face, and that, combined with her profession, gave him reason to hope she could keep her head in a crisis. He slipped his pistol in his pocket—it would be easier to yank it out of there than to draw it from inside the coat—and touched the dome. It split and melted away, and he slipped the sleep ring off her wavy dyed-blond hair.

Sally's eyes snapped open, and she gasped. Afraid that she was about to cry out, he pressed his hand over her mouth.

"Don't scream!" he said. He'd forgotten how spooky his voice would sound, and it startled him. "I'm here to help you. Nod if you understand."

She did, and he took his hand away. "Dr. Umbra," she said.

He started to say, no, he wasn't, then decided not to waste the time. Explanations–especially demoralizing ones involving the news that two superheroes were dead–could wait until they were all safe.

"The aliens took you all prisoner," he said. "Just touch the cover on top of a slab and it'll open. Then pull the ring off the person's head, and he'll wake up. But we have to be quiet, so the creatures don't overhear."

She sat up. "I understand." Then a boom and jolt made her jump. "What was *that?*"

"One of the reasons we need to hurry."

She did, and so did the people the two of them woke next. It only took a few minutes to get everybody up.

Up, but not, in all cases, in control of themselves. A skinny woman with lots of turquoise jewelry and fingernails painted to match–part of Germantown's art scene, by the look of her–suddenly broke down sobbing.

Sally put her hand on her shoulder. "Please," she said, "we have to be quiet, or the aliens will hear."

The other woman sobbed louder. "I saw one of them," she said. "It was *hideous!*"

Matt strode over to her, grabbed her by the throat, and jerked her up on tiptoe. Her eyes opened wide with shock, and Sally looked almost equally taken aback. All the whispered conversations in the cell stopped abruptly.

"Shut up," Matt growled. "Or I'll shut you up permanently. Because you are *not* going to ruin everyone else's chances of getting out of here. Do you understand?"

The artsy woman nodded like a bobble head, and he decided he could let her go. For the moment, anyway, she was more scared of him–or of Dr. Umbra's sinister persona–than she was of the wasps.

He looked and decided they were all about as ready as they were going to get. "All right," he said, pulling the gun from his pocket. "I'm going to scout a little way ahead. Stop when I signal you to stop, move when I wave you on, and *keep quiet.* Anytime you can't see me, Sally the nurse here is in charge. Any questions?" Apparently there weren't. "Then let's go."

He led them down the passageway. They were trying to be quiet, he could tell that, but every creak of shoe leather or rustle of clothing seemed horribly loud even so, and whenever the next blast and shock startled a gasp out of someone, or made one person lurch into another, it was worse. Gritting his teeth, Matt told himself they were nowhere near as noisy as they seemed. It was just his nerves that made it feel that way.

The confidence invisibility had given him was gone. In fact, he'd never felt more out of his depth. Why couldn't there have been a cop among the prisoners? Why hadn't there been a Navy SEA–

A wasp came out of an archway several feet in front of him. Perhaps because it was alone, it wasn't buzzing, and thus hadn't given any warning of its presence.

Startled, Matt froze. The alien whirled in his direction and extended a segmented arm. It had something made of metal and crystal affixed among the twitching, scissoring appendages that served it for a hand.

"Shoot!" Sally called.

The cry spurred him into motion; he pointed Dr. Umbra's pistol and pulled the trigger. There was no bang, no kick, and no flash as such, just the pulse of shadow he'd noticed when the vigilante was shooting. But, with a sort of wet, cracking thump, something smashed the alien's head to pulp, and the creature flopped over on its side.

Matt had never killed anything bigger than a normal bug, certainly not anything intelligent, and for an instant, he was horrified at the gruesome thing he'd done. But that feeling quickly gave way to a kind of angry satisfaction. Because after what they'd done to Dr. Umbra, Red Bear, and who knew how many others, the invaders had it coming. And because he now knew the pistols would work for him. They'd work pretty darn well. If he absolutely had to, he could do more than just sneak around.

Seemingly unfazed by the monstrous appearance of the wasp, Sally hurried forward, probably so she could talk to Matt without raising her voice. "Do you think the other creatures heard?" she asked.

Jeez! Why wasn't *he* already trying to determine that? "I should give the outfit to you," he muttered.

"What?"

"Nothing." He listened and didn't hear any buzzing. "I think we're okay. The aliens are hearing a lot of bangs and thuds. That was just one more."

"Good." She stooped beside the wasp's body and pulled loose the weapon it had pointed at Matt, essentially a flanged tube mounted on a bracelet.

"Can you see how to work it?" he asked.

"I see three buttons," she said, slipping the gadget onto her wrist. "One of them is probably the trigger."

"Well, don't mess around with it unless you have to. Get the others moving again while I see what's ahead."

He explored more corridors and looked into more rooms, some containing objects and devices so strange that he couldn't even guess at their purposes. He hit a dead end and had to double back. Then he heard more buzzing. A lot of it, actually.

His immediate impulse was to turn around and go the other way. But then his intuition—or maybe it was just his desperation—told him it might be worth finding out *exactly* what was up ahead. He raised his hand to tell his companions to halt, then willed himself invisible and stalked onward.

The corridor ended in a room with a high ceiling, a jagged hole with blackened edges in the far wall, and gray sky showing on the other side of it. That was the good news. The bad was that several wasps were crawling around the breach working to patch it, and several more were peering out with devices like rifles in their grips. The latter were presumably guards stationed here to keep enemies from entering through the hole.

Matt turned, tiptoed away, reappeared, and took stock of his power level. It wasn't great news, either. The tank was almost half empty already. Evidently invisibility did take a lot of juice. He hoped the pistols drew less.

He rejoined his companions, gathered them in close, and explained what he'd discovered. "It's the first–"

A boom and jolt interrupted him.

"–way out we've found. We have to go for it. We can't just wander around in here until the aliens catch us."

"But if they're right there," said a stocky black man in a red blazer and piano-key tie, "if they're *armed*–"

"Dr. Umbra is a superhero," Sally said. "He'll take care of them."

Yeah, right. Except that *was* the plan, wasn't it? No matter how incompetent Matt felt, he couldn't think of anything better to try.

"This is what we're going to do," he said. "I'll go on ahead like I did before. When you hear a...commotion start, run after me and go out the hole. Then run some more. Don't stop for anything."

Sally gave him a brisk nod. "We understand. Right, people?"

The others murmured in agreement.

Matt realized there was nothing more to say. His pulse throbbing in his neck, he turned in a swirl of cloak, headed back toward the buzzing, and willed himself invisible halfway there.

The room with the breach was as he'd left it, which he supposed was better than if he'd come back to find all the aliens lined up with their guns pointed at him. He took a breath, aimed his pistol at one of the sentry wasps, and pulled the trigger.

The shot smashed in the creature's thorax, and it fell down thrashing. The buzzing swelled. The insects had been talking; now they were shouting to one another.

Matt shifted his aim and fired. The blast severed a wasp's leg and blew its abdomen and stinger away from the rest of it in a splash of gore. It fell down heaving and flailing, too. A small, squeamish part of him wished he could kill the creatures cleanly. But there was no time to fret about that or much of anything else.

The aliens pivoted this way and that, looking for their enemy. Another boom shook the fortress. Despite the whine of buzzing wings, Matt heard pounding feet. He glanced back and saw that in another moment, the first of his fellow prisoners would burst into the room.

And find wasps still blocking the way out, unless Matt did something about it. He fired at one of the workers, and the shot tore it loose from the ragged edge of the breach and hurled it outside. He shot at another, missed, and only pounded a dent in the wall. Still, the remaining laborers scrambled and leaped away from the opening to join the sentries on the floor. Unfortunately, they all had bracelet guns like the one Sally had scavenged.

Of course, like the guards, they couldn't shoot what they couldn't see. Too bad that had to change. Because Matt had no doubt the aliens would blast the other escapees unless he provided a more attractive target.

He willed himself visible, fired, and shouted, "Hey, shitheads! Over here!" He had the feeling his real voice broke like a teenager's, but Dr. Umbra's didn't.

The wasps pivoted. He vanished and flung himself sideways. Blue rays stabbed through the space he'd just vacated.

He reappeared, shot, disappeared, dodged. Did it again and then again. *No pattern,* he told himself, *don't fall into a pattern. Don't let them guess where you're going to jump.*

With his attention locked on the creatures trying to kill him, he was only marginally aware of the other prisoners dashing behind the wasps to cross the chamber. But he caught it when somebody shrilled, "It's too high!" and Sally snapped, "Hang by your hands and drop!" He also noticed when a guy in his twenties like him, a guy who could have *been* him, evidently got too close to an alien, and, provoked, the invader left off trying to shoot Matt to spin around and fire at the other human instead. The guy pitched forward onto his face.

Matt made a point of shooting that wasp next.

He could pick his target because, to his own amazement, he was holding his own. He doubted his fighting looked all that much like the flickering, nimble dance he'd watched Dr. Umbra perform, but even his beginner's use of invisibility kept the insects from hitting him, while the shots from the vigilante's raygun smashed them one by one.

I can win this! he thought. *I can live through it!* He fired, vanished, sidestepped. Reappeared, found a wasp, shot it. Then a deafening boom made the floor buck and knocked him off balance. He reeled backward, glancing up in the process, and saw an alien swooping down at him, the arm with the bracelet gun extended.

He realized what had happened. The creature had crawled up the wall, clung to the ceiling, and waited for a good moment to take him by surprise. And it had found one. Even going invisible wouldn't protect him while he had no equilibrium and couldn't dodge.

Still floundering, he tried to point his own gun. Fired. Missed.

But somebody else didn't. A blue ray stabbed into the wasp. It convulsed, fell, and smacked down on the floor.

Finally recovering his balance, Matt pivoted, looking for the next threat. There wasn't one. There was only Sally, standing by the hole in the wall, her arm and bracelet gun outstretched.

"Thanks," he panted.

She strode to the guy who'd reminded Matt of himself and kneeled down beside him. She put her hand in front of his nostrils and mouth, touched two fingers to the side of his neck, and then started CPR. Matt looked on for a second, then remembered they were still in danger and turned to watch the door instead.

To his relief, no new wasps came rushing down the corridor. And after a little while, Sally said, "I can't tell how the beam killed him, but he's gone. I imagine they all are."

Matt looked around and belatedly noticed the other four human bodies sprawled on the floor. "Damn it!"

As she stood up, Sally said, "You did as much as anyone could."

No. Not as much as the real Dr. Umbra could have. But it still wasn't the time or place to go into that.

"We need to go," he said, and they hurried to the breach.

Now that he was right in front of the hole, and it didn't have wasps crawling all over it, Matt could see that the aliens' fort stood on top of one of the Little League diamonds in Ballantine Park, and that this particular part of it was about fifteen feet above the infield. The other prisoners were scurrying away in a ragged line.

And, thank God, no aliens were chasing them or shooting at them.

Sally hung by her hands and dropped, and then Matt did the same. They caught up with their fellow escapees in a stand of oaks about a hundred yards away, where the others had evidently stopped to catch their breath. He turned around, took his first look at the fort from the outside, and gasped.

The structure was a bulbous mass several stories tall that reminded him of a hornet's nest or beehive. None of the aliens inside had any attention to spare for escaping prisoners because of the figure flying overhead. Despite the intervening distance, Matt could just make out the gleam of silver and cobalt blue armor and the beams of rippling distortion stabbing down from the hero's gauntlets. Dr. Umbra and Red Bear were gone, but Magnetar was still fighting to protect the city!

Specifically, he was trying to blast the hive-fort to pieces. Sometimes, his energy beams struck it to no apparent effect, neutralized by a force field, maybe, not that Matt really knew what a force field was. But sometimes they hit with a crash, punching holes, breaking pieces loose, and no doubt producing the shocks he and his companions had experienced while inside.

Meanwhile, rays flashed up from artillery hidden in the outer walls, and from the airships and flying wasps maneuvering around the hive. But, swerving and zigzagging, Magnetar dodged most of them, and the couple that hit him didn't appear to bother him.

Matt's companions started cheering the superhero on, and he felt the same swell of hope. It lasted half a minute, until a second hive plunged down from the layer of cloud overhead with its own contingent of airships and insect soldiers swirling around it.

Matt supposed the hive on the baseball diamond had been able to fly, too, before Magnetar damaged it and forced it to the ground. Unfortunately, it could still fight, and now, suddenly, the superhero was caught between it and a fresh one with all its capabilities intact.

The armored man tried to simultaneously rocket out of the box and do barrel rolls to shoot at both threats. Blue lights pulsed across the surfaces of the hives as their artillery fired back. Matt didn't actually see any rays hit Magnetar. It was harder to make them out in the daylight, even on a sunless morning like this. But something must have, because a haze that looked like pixelation suddenly seethed around the hero, and then he fell out of the sky.

It was a long way down. Matt's companions had time to cry out in denial and horror before their champion crashed to earth.

Instantly, wasps swooped down around their fallen enemy. Matt wished for Magnetar to spring to his feet and blast them to pieces like the invincible superhuman he was supposed to be. But that didn't happen.

"We're all dead," someone said, his voice as gray as the day itself.

"No!" Sally said. "There are still heroes left! There's one right here!"

No! Matt thought. He'd been insanely lucky up to now, but this had to stop. He was no superhero, had no idea how to be, and didn't want the responsibility.

He wanted to run his store and get promoted to regional manager. Shoot hoops and play video games with his friends. Find somebody new to date now that his last relationship had run its course. Attend his high school reunion the first weekend of next month.

But who was he kidding? That pleasant, ordinary life was gone, maybe forever. The invaders had–what was the sci-fi word?–*disintegrated* it with their rays. And in this grim new existence that had taken his place, he found he wasn't heartless enough to rob Sally and the people clustered around her of the only hope they had.

"We need to keep moving," he said in Dr. Umbra's ghostly whisper. "Find a place to lie low."

And with that he led them onward, out of the park and into the shattered, smoking ruins of Jackson City. The huge wasps buzzed and flitted overhead.

The Enemy of My Enemy

Matt stuck his head up out of the hole in the attic ceiling and checked the sky. He didn't see any wasps or wasp-machines. So he tested what was left of the charred, sagging roof, decided it could still support his weight, and climbed out on top of it.

He was getting better at climbing and picking his way through unsafe buildings. Better at sneaking and scavenging. Better, he thought bitterly, at living like a rat in the ruins of the city.

What he hadn't improved at was telling the truth. He still hadn't explained to Sally, the other prisoners he'd rescued, or the survivors they'd met since that he wasn't Dr. Umbra. He still didn't have the heart to reveal they didn't have a superhero on their side, even if said hero wasn't attempting anything more ambitious than finding food, water, supplies, and good places to hide.

Because what other hope did they have? With no TV, phones, or Internet, it was impossible to know for sure, but it certainly seemed like nobody from outside was coming to rescue Jackson City. Nobody could, not if the aliens had attacked the rest of the planet as successfully as they had here.

Still, Matt wasn't sure it was right to lie and give people *false* hope, and even if it was, it was *lonely*. A superhero couldn't say he was scared, sad, and confused. He couldn't even unmask and show his face. It was no use pretending to be Dr. Umbra unless his behavior was consistent with the vigilante's cold, relentless, and spooky reputation.

Matt scowled and told himself to man up. Who cared how he *felt* when so many people were *dead?* The streets and blasted buildings were full of them, and unless he wanted his friends and himself added to the body count, he needed to take care of business.

Which, at the moment, was scouting the downed hive-ship in Ballantine Park. Now that the similar vessel that had helped to kill Magnetar had flown away to parts unknown, this was the biggest alien structure in the city—or at least in the parts Matt had managed to visit—and still a hub of constant activity. Flyers were always coming and going while other wasps crawled around on the walls.

So it seemed worth keeping an eye on the thing. Fortunately, since he'd discovered that the black one-way lenses in Dr. Umbra's mask could function like night-vision goggles, binoculars, or both at the same time, he could observe it from a distance.

He clambered to the crest of the roof, kneeled behind a broken stub of chimney, and peered at the hive. After an instant, the mask somehow knew to magnify it, and it seemed to leap at him.

Matt's eyes narrowed. There were only a couple wasps crawling on the hive-ship tonight. That could be bad, because the creatures had been workers making repairs. Their absence might mean the work was done, and while he couldn't guess the full implications of that, he doubted he was going to like them.

Something buzzed. He jumped, but only a little, because the noise was soft and thus distant, not the piercing, oscillating whine one heard when the wasps were flying or communicating close by.

The broken roof shivered beneath him.

He jerked around.

A wasp crouched at the opposite end of the ridge. Despite the shadowy camouflage Dr. Umbra's costume provided, the creature's round black eyes were staring straight at Matt, and it held an energy rifle in the complicated tangles of pincers and segmented finger-like growths that served as its hands.

Matt reacted as he'd learned to react. He willed himself invisible, jumped up, and dodged.

Or rather, he tried. In the desperation of the moment, he'd forgotten where he was. The pitch of the roof threw him off balance, and while he was reeling, his foot caught on something sticking up from the charred, broken surface.

He fell on his side and slid headfirst, his body tearing loose shingles along the way. The four-storey drop waiting at the edge of the roof felt like it was rushing to meet him.

He scrabbled and clutched, trying to seize hold of anything that would arrest his descent. His right hand dropped into a hole, and then, a split second later, bumped what felt like a length of exposed rafter.

He grabbed it with all his strength. The sudden stop jolted his arm all the way up to the shoulder, but what mattered was that he *did* stop. For an instant, he felt a surge of relief, and then he remembered the wasp.

I'm invisible! he thought, and immediately knew it was stupid. Scraping shingles loose had left a trail with him at the end of it. The wasp knew exactly where he was, and sure enough, when he twisted his head, it was already aiming at him.

He flung himself rolling to the side, and, with a hiss, a thin blue beam burned a hole in the section of roof he'd just vacated. The damaged surface bounced beneath him, and, missing him as narrowly as the first, the alien's second and third shots made it clear that it could still track him without difficulty.

His only hope was to shoot back, and he stuck his hand in the pocket of Dr. Umbra's caped coat. For a terrifying moment, he thought the pistol had fallen out, but then his fingers found it.

Then a section of roof collapsed beneath his tumbling weight. He plummeted amid a shower of shingles and splinters and slammed down on the floor of the attic.

It knocked the wind out of him. As he gasped in a breath, the wasp flew over the hole he'd just made and hovered. It pointed the energy rifle at him.

He jerked up his hand and shot. Darkness pulsed from the end of his pistol, and invisible force ripped through the insect's thorax, tearing the two wings on the left away from the body.

At the same moment, the creature fired back. The blue pulse burned into the floor beside Matt, and then the insect dropped on top of him, stunning him all over again. Its abdomen flexed repeatedly, trying to stab him with the stinger but fortunately only hammering the floor. Until the wasp finally shuddered and stopped moving.

Shaking with revulsion and leftover adrenaline, Matt dragged himself out from under the carcass, and, mindful of his power level, willed himself to reappear. The wasp's bodily fluids trickled down from his cloak. Dr. Umbra's costume was apparently waterproof and stain-resistant, and it was a good thing. Washing clothes was no longer easy, and dry cleaning was pretty much out of the question.

Matt stuck his head out of the hole he'd just fallen through. As far as he could tell, no other wasps were rushing to his location. The thing he'd just killed had apparently thought sneaking up on him and shooting him in the back was a better idea than calling for reinforcements.

It had almost worked, too. Which raised the question, how had this wasp been so stealthy, anyway? How could it fly without buzzing loudly when he was pretty sure the rest of its kind couldn't?

Now that he was thinking about it, he realized there were other peculiarities. A normal wasp had red and black stripes and had trouble seeing him in the dark. This one was all black, and although Matt had no way of knowing how difficult it had been, the thing had sure as hell spotted him.

"Why is this one different?" he muttered.

"Hypothesis," replied a voice, making him jump, "the extraterrestrials have bioengineered a variant, possibly for the specific purpose of hunting you."

By the time the voice finished its statement, Matt had recognized its calm, intellectual baritone, not that doing so was entirely reassuring. The only other time he'd heard it, it had inflicted excruciating pain on him and threatened to kill him before falling silent as mysteriously as it had started talking.

"Who are you?" Matt asked. And, even more importantly: "Are we officially on the same side now?"

"Assessing," said the voice. It paused for a moment. "Aside from bruises and contusions, you appear uninjured. Conjecture: As a result of my extended silence, you suspect I am not the real Solomon, or that I have been compromised. For this reason, you have resorted to a duplicitous mode of interaction."

It took a moment for Matt to sort that out, and once he did, he was reluctant to ask the question that came to mind. Maybe it was better to leave well enough alone.

But maybe not, too. If, as he hoped, Solomon had useful things to tell him, he—or it?—might be *more* helpful if he understood Matt's actual situation.

So he took a deep breath, mentally crossed his fingers, and asked, "Do you think I'm the real Dr. Umbra?"

"Why would I not?"

"Because the first time, you figured out right away that I wasn't. Don't you remember talking to me before?"

"Assessing." Pause. "That memory is not currently accessible. I sustained damage during the initial attack. Parts of me shift on- and offline as I attempt repairs." Pause. "As you are not Dr. Umbra, you must divest yourself of his costume—"

"Stop! Don't threaten me, and for God's sake, don't zap me! We've already been through this. Dr. Umbra is dead. You saw his body. I've been using his stuff to help other people and stay alive myself. But I'll be glad to hand it over to whoever is supposed to get it."

"Assessing. At this time, it is unclear to whom you might pass the equipment."

Shit. Matt had guessed right. There was nobody left to rescue Jackson City, or if there was, the voice knew nothing about it.

His neck tightened and his shoulders ached with a fresh upwelling of grief and frustration. And at that very moment, like the aliens had timed it to push him even closer to despair, the hive-ship rose back up into the air.

Maybe it was leaving. That could be good. But even as he imagined it, Matt's instincts warned him it was just wishful thinking. And sure enough, the hive came to a stop high above the ground. It ended up close to the crescent moon, like it was positioning itself to blast that to pieces as well.

"An aerial position enhances the extraterrestrials' ability to monitor the city," Solomon said. "It also makes it more difficult for a hostile force to assault them."

"I get that," Matt replied. "Although there's nobody left to assault them anyway."

"I have been unable to reestablish contact with Red Bear and Magnetar. This, however, is not without precedent. It would be premature–"

"No. It wouldn't. I saw them die." An instant after the words left his mouth, Matt regretted the bluntness with which he'd delivered the news. By now, he was pretty sure he was talking to a machine, but that didn't necessarily mean Solomon didn't have feelings. He'd heard of robots and androids that supposedly did. "I'm sorry."

"As am I," said Solomon, although his tone remained as dispassionate as before. "But it would be an error to allow dismay to divert us from present concerns."

"Which I guess are getting to know each other. I'm Matt, you're Solomon, and I'm guessing you're a computer."

"In essence. I am a dispersed artificial intelligence designed to facilitate the endeavors of the superheroes of Jackson City. My existence was a secret, but the extraterrestrials either discovered it and sought to eliminate me or else I simply came to harm in the general bombardment of the city."

"Well, I'm glad it didn't kill you. Since you worked with Dr. Umbra and have a link to his costume, can you tell me how things work?"

"Yes. The equipment is based on Lemurian technology. It stores dark energy via an attractor comparable to a Sachs-Lemaitre micro-anomaly detector and–"

"Stop!" Matt said. "I'm already lost. I'm not a scientist, and I don't need to know the science. I need to understand how to *use* the equipment."

"Understood," Solomon said, "although you indicated you already have been using it."

"Well, some of it's easy. The camo effect is just there all the time. The mask automatically gives me the kind of vision I need. The guns shoot, and all I have to do to go invisible is want it. Although that drains the battery really fast."

"Because shunting light around you in an undetectable fashion while still allowing you to see and move normally requires considerable energy. The amount needed to discharge concussive force through the pistols is trivial by comparison."

"If you say so. One of the things I *can't* do is make the pistols jump from the holsters into my hands. I copied the move Dr. Umbra made, but nothing happened."

"You have to curl your fingers and think the command *guns* simultaneously. Dr. Umbra didn't want the pistols teleporting every time he attempted to use his hands or thought about firearms."

"Okay." Mat returned both pistols, the one still in his right hand and the one in his left coat pocket, to their holsters inside the garment. Then he flexed his black-gloved fingers and thought *gun.*

The pistol appeared instantly, and, even though that was what was supposed to happen, he almost fumbled the catch, almost pulled the trigger, too, before he had hold of the weapon properly. He hoped Solomon hadn't noticed but figured he probably had.

"You can teleport both pistols at once," the artificial intelligence said. "That was Dr. Umbra's accustomed method."

"Because he trained to shoot them both at the same time. I haven't. I'm lucky I've done some target shooting and paintball, or I probably couldn't hit anything with one."

"Understood. To return the pistol to the holster, loosen your grip and think the command *holster* simultaneously."

Matt did, the gun vanished, and he immediately felt its weight riding under his arm. Smiling, he made the weapon jump back and forth several more times.

"I think I've got it," he said.

"I concur," Solomon replied, and then white light flashed off to the east, beyond the floating hive-ship and the far edge of the park.

Matt peered but couldn't figure out what had made the flash. It had been a fair way off, even for Dr. Umbra's augmented vision, and there were buildings in the way.

"Do you know what that was?" he asked.

"Unable to determine," Solomon replied. "At this point in my repair process, I perceive only what you perceive."

More lights flickered. Initially, they were blue, and then the white one flashed again.

Learning how to make the pistols jump into his hands had lifted Matt's spirits, but this new development made them soar. "Somebody's fighting the wasps," he said.

"We cannot be certain of that," Solomon replied.

"Sure we can! The blue flashes are the wasps' rayguns, and the white one is...somebody else's weapon." He turned and strode for the folding dropdown stairs that connected the attic to the rest of the apartment building.

"What is your intention?" Solomon asked.

"What do you think?" Matt scrambled down the stairs. "I'm going to go link up with the good guys. Help them if they need it."

"I recommend caution and reiterate: We actually know little about the situation."

"Then help me be as prepared as possible when I get there." Matt trotted toward the stairs at the end of the corridor. The door to one of the apartments was open, and a woman's bloated, stinking corpse lay half in and half out. He veered around it.

"I will assist however I can."

"Dr. Umbra's other big trick was walking through walls, or having bullets and beams from rayguns go right through him. How do I do that?"

"Assessing." Solomon fell silent until Matt cracked out the door on the ground floor and peered out to make certain nothing was lying in wait. Then: "The cloak is damaged."

Matt remembered the barrage of rays that had hit the vigilante in the back. "So it doesn't have that power anymore?"

"Not presently," the artificial intelligence said. "I may be able to repair it. However…"

Matt gave it a couple seconds and then asked, "'However,' what?"

Solomon didn't answer, either because he'd moved on to a self-repair procedure that had broken their connection or because something worse had happened.

"Damn it," Matt muttered, and then put the computer out of his mind. It was aggravating to lose contact, but he still had the battle to investigate. With luck, it would turn out to be more important anyway.

He trotted to a silver-gray Prius with a shattered windshield, dented hood, and dried blood all over the front seat. Matt had needed to drag the driver's corpse from behind the wheel before claiming the car for his own.

It wasn't exactly an Umbramobile. Maybe there was such a vehicle, something long and black and dark energy-powered, stashed away somewhere, and maybe Solomon could direct him to it if the computer ever spoke again. Meanwhile, Matt needed *something* to get around, and the Prius ran quietly. It was also good on gas, which was important now that filling up had become a risky, complicated business.

He climbed in, pushed the Start button, and pulled away from the curb without turning on the headlights. With his mask, he didn't need them and definitely didn't need what they might attract.

The cool night air blew in through the broken windshield. He tugged Dr. Umbra's slouch hat a little lower on his head.

*

Peering from a sixth-story window, Clarence Harvey divided his attention between the sky and the dozen captives standing around the fires flickering in the trashcans in the middle of the intersection. He'd ordered the prisoners to stay close to the barrels to make sure the wavering yellow glow would light them up. They kept shying away, though. They understood they were bait, and that when they lured something in, the fires would be ground zero.

What they apparently *didn't* understand was that they should be more scared of Clarence and the other WMDs than they were of bugs from outer space. Scowling, he lifted his bullhorn to remind them.

He was still choosing his words when they scattered in all directions.

Clarence felt a spasm of rage. It clutched him again a moment later when some of his own pet normals opened fire from other windows. Their AK-47's rattled, and a woman fell down.

"Stop shooting!" Clarence thundered through the bullhorn. If the idiots slaughtered all the bait, they'd have to start all over rounding up more.

The assault rifles fell silent. That left the superpowered members of the gang with the chore of stopping the prisoners from getting away.

White light flashed, power crackled, and a fat guy danced a spastic dance and fell down. Sweet Lady Q had used her power to tase him.

Red light danced on a teenage girl. Though its specific effects were unpredictable, Freakmaker's power usually crippled the target, and that was what happened now. Her legs crumpling beneath her like the bones had melted, the girl collapsed in a heap.

Two down, but the rest were still scurrying. As usual, Clarence thought, it was up to him.

He reached out to parked, disabled, and abandoned cars in the fugitives' paths. He could feel the steel inside them, and it could feel him. That was part of what made him Death Metal.

His will sent the cars flipping and crashing end over end toward the captives running in their directions. For an instant, Clarence flashed on Indiana Jones running from the rolling boulder. That was a good movie, although it had annoyed him when he realized the villains were going to be Nazis. People didn't understand the Nazis. If they'd read *Mein Kampf* or Nietzche, maybe they would.

Some of the running people froze, and Clarence had to slow or stop tumbling cars to keep from crushing them. Others turned and ran back the way they'd come. A couple brave ones tried to dodge around the threat, and he flipped and jerked the vehicles from side to side to cut them off.

Gradually, he herded all the prisoners who were still on their feet back into the intersection. Two of his soldiers in their Army Surplus urban camo dragged the fat man and crippled girl back.

Clarence pulled metal from his surroundings. Pipes jumped out of the wall, and handles ripped off desk drawers. A pair of gray file cabinets lurched in his direction.

All the objects dissolved into dust before they could reach him, and then the powder stuck to his skin and built up a layer of armor. It also drove roots like tiny wires inward, permeating and transforming his flesh. It didn't hurt. In fact, it was an exhilarating, almost sexual tingle.

It was hard to control other metal objects when he was armored up, but that didn't worry him. He doubted he'd need to roll the cars around anymore. The captives were intimidated now, although not as intimidated as they were going to be.

He leaped out the window and slammed down in the street. The landing knocked him down on one knee but didn't hurt. His shell protected him.

Savoring their trembling and the fear in their faces, he advanced on the prisoners. "What did I order you to do?" he asked.

They all just stared at him like the frightened sheep they were.

"Somebody had better speak up," he said, "or I'm going to start executing people. So, anyone? Anyone? Bueller?"

"T-to stay by the fires," stammered a chunky Asian guy with a square, grimy face. His left arm was broken, and someone had splinted it with a piece of broom handle.

Clarence smiled at him. "Bingo. But *somebody* in the group thought it would be smart to disobey. Whose bright idea was it?"

The teary eyes of the girl with the boneless legs shifted away from the guilty party. So did those of a youngish guy in khakis and a nylon windbreaker.

So now Clarence knew, but it wasn't enough to read their tells. He needed them to obey his every command and answer his every question, even when it meant ratting out a friend.

He looked down at the newly crippled girl. "Freakmaker changed you," he said, "and he can change you back. If I tell him to."

The girl clenched herself and squinched her eyes shut.

"Suit yourself." He willed the metal sheathing his fingers to elongate and sharpen itself into claws. Then he swung at the girl's head, which both *crunched* and *squished* as it broke. She probably died without ever knowing it was happening. But the other captives knew. They cringed, gasped, and whimpered.

"Okay, then," Clarence said, pivoting back toward the man with the broken arm. "You were smart before. Can you be smart again?"

"You don't have to tell," quavered the instigator. He was a lanky, middle-aged man well on his way to baldness. He had on a stained, rumpled business suit but had ditched the tie. "It was me. I'm responsible. Please don't hurt anyone else."

Clarence didn't like it that the ringleader had revealed himself. It made the son of a bitch look too much like a hero. But he hid his displeasure with a leer. "You'll never know if I do or don't," he said, raising his gory claws and stepping into striking distance.

Then, overhead, something buzzed, and the AK-47's clattered. Clarence looked up.

A single wasp-shaped alien airship–or robot, there was really no way to tell–was hovering over the intersection. Clarence's plan had worked, except that he wasn't supposed to be standing out in the open with the bait.

A brilliant flash lit up the street, and for a second, a loud crackle covered the whine of the flying thing. Sweet Lady Q had thrown a full-power bolt of electricity.

The flyer lurched and rolled, then righted itself. Blue light pulsed from various points along its body as it returned fire.

Glowing like a white paper bag with a candle burning inside, sparks falling from her outstretched fingertips, Sweet Lady Q vanished from her window. Still blinking from her lightning flash, Clarence couldn't tell if the rays had hit her or if she'd dodged and avoided them.

He *did* know he couldn't do much against the flyer where and how he was. He ran for the shelter of the office building where he'd stationed himself before, and the captives bolted, too. Unfortunately, that included Mr. Businessman. Clarence almost turned back around to kill him but knew it would be stupid.

Electricity flared and crackled. Sweet Lady Q was still in the fight. An instant later, something roared loud enough to shatter windows. It was Svergr's favorite heavy weapon, the one he called the Bear Killer.

Clarence scrambled through the revolving door he'd broken into previously, then willed away his armor. It fell away with a hiss and left him standing in gray powder. The next time the flying machine swooped low enough for him to see, he tried to lock onto it with his power.

No dice. The flyer was made of metal, or at least had metal in it, but not a kind he'd practiced on before, and on top of that, it was simply buzzing around too fast.

He'd have to use the cars as he had before. He grabbed the nearest, waited for the flyer to reappear, and heaved his chosen weapon—a Nissan Optima, now so crumpled it was almost un-recognizable—with all his might.

The hurtling car smashed into the flyer just as another blast from the Bear Killer slammed into it from the opposite side. One of the crystalline wings shattered, and the alien machine and Clarence's missile dropped together to slam down in the street.

The crash was deafening, and in contrast, the silence that followed, as Sweet Lady Q, Svergr, and the riflemen all stopped shooting, seemed equally resonant and profound. Then a hatch in the top of the flyer blew away from the fuselage and a lone wasp crawled out.

The loose ends of his black sash flying, Zhang Sanfeng in-stantly leaped from a third-story window. The kid arguably wasn't a super at all, just a really good athlete, and maybe as a result, he was always frantic to prove himself. He landed, rolled, flipped back onto his feet, and charged the wasp with a short, curved sword in either hand.

The wasp aimed its energy rifle at him. He leaped above the beam, somersaulted, and came down slashing. His blades spat-tered gore through the air, and the insect fell down and thrashed. Its stinger stabbed, but, making the move look casual, Zhang simply stepped back out of range and watched it die.

And for a moment, Clarence imagined that was that. Then three more ships appeared above the rooftops.

*

By the time he reached the far side of the park, Matt could hear buzzing, crackling, crashing, and the popping of gunfire.

That pretty much clinched it that the battle was happening on the west side of the business district, which was to say, just a few blocks away.

Because the aliens had originally attacked late at night, there weren't too many wrecked or abandoned vehicles in the middle of the streets. Matt didn't have to bump up onto the sidewalk or backtrack often, but every such delay made his muscles tighten in impatience.

When he spotted the wasp-things flitting above the roof-tops of the office buildings, he pulled over. Dr. Umbra's stealth wouldn't hide him if he drove into the middle of the battle in a Toyota.

His heart thumping, he climbed out of the car, started to reach into his pocket, remembered, and commanded a pistol to jump into his hand instead. He considered going invisible but decided, *Not yet.*

Sticking close to the row of buildings beside him, taking advantage of the deeper darkness at their feet, he crept forward. He peeked around a corner and discovered he'd been even nearer to the fight than he'd realized. It was raging right in front of him.

Three alien airships lay crashed in the street, metal parts crumpled, crystal wings and "eyes" broken into jagged, glittering pieces. A pair of wasps crawled out of an opening in one of the vessels, and a man in a blue outfit with a kind of black do-rag mask, a sash, and a Chinese character written on the back of the tunic charged them. Almost faster than Matt could see, the guy slashed then to pieces with a pair of machete-like blades.

Glowing white like an angel, sparks falling from her body, a slender woman in a bodysuit leaned far out of a window to point her hand at the one ship still in the air. A dazzling bolt of electricity sizzled from her fingertips and burned through the vessel. It fell, breaking to pieces as it plummeted, and she jerked inside just in time to keep one of the larger scraps from bashing her head in.

The banging and clatter when the rubble hit the street was painfully loud. Afterward, everything was quiet while the humans waited for wasps to come out of the newly downed ship. Eventually, though, when nothing emerged, the riflemen in the windows started cheering. Matt almost felt like joining in.

But he didn't, because even though he was no expert on superheroes and supervillains, he was pretty sure he recognized this bunch as a gang of the latter known as the WMDs. The woman who threw lightning bolts was Sweet Lady Q, the middle-aged man coming out of a revolving door in a gold panel shirt, silver jodhpurs, and a wide copper belt and boots was Death Metal, the leader, and the swordsman was...some kung fu guy. Matt was lucky he remembered two of the names.

Whatever they called themselves, it was a safe bet Dr. Umbra had hunted them and tried to put them in jail. The question was, did that matter anymore?

"Solomon?" Matt whispered. "Are you there? I need your advice."

But the AI still wasn't talking. Great.

Matt took a deep breath, willed himself invisible, and then skulked toward Death Metal, who was heading for the crashed airships like many of his crew.

"Freeze," Matt said, the mask converting his voice into Dr. Umbra's menacing whisper. Death Metal stopped walking. "I have my gun on you."

"Dr. Umbra," the supervillain replied, sounding surprised but not alarmed. "I spoke to a witness who swore the wasps got you when they took down Red Bear."

"I escaped."

By now, Death Metal's underlings realized something was wrong. Frowning, the masked swordsman started toward him.

"Tell them to stay back," Matt said.

Death Metal raised his hand. "Everyone, keep your distance and don't do anything stupid. Dr. Umbra is here, and he has me covered."

"He won't kill you," the kung fu fighter said.

"Two weeks ago," said Death Metal, "I *might* have been willing to bet my life on that. But it's a new world now, isn't it, Doctor? And you were always less squeamish than your friends."

"Much less," said Matt; it seemed like a creepy Dr. Umbra kind of thing to say. "But I don't want to kill you."

"Or arrest me either, I assume. Where would you put me?"

"Nowhere, and that's the point. It *is* a new world, where there aren't criminals or crime fighters anymore. There's just us humans against the wasps, and the best way to defeat them is to join forces."

Death Metal snorted. "You want to join the WMDs?"

"I want an alliance. We can help each other, and we need to. As far as I can tell, we're the only supers left."

"I guess you haven't made it over to the East Side. Krymzon Red and the Blood Machine are still around." Matt had heard of that gang, too, but knew even less about them than the WMDs. "Still, I see your point."

Matt checked his internal meter. He'd burned through half his charge. He could stay invisible for a while longer, but not forever.

"Then do we have a deal?" he asked.

"Yes," said Death Metal, "strange as it seems, we do. Show yourself, and I'll explain it to the others."

Matt glanced at the gang members who, though they'd kept their distance as ordered, were watching their leader intently, just waiting for a chance to act. In addition to the swordsman, there was Sweet Lady Q, glowing and sticking to a wall fifteen feet off the ground. A figure whose bulky asymmetrical armor looked like he'd pieced it together in a junkyard. A handsome guy who, despite the omnipresent dirt and dust, was so sharply groomed and dressed that he might have stepped off a *GQ* cover except for the red luminescence rippling on his fingertips like phosphorescent nail polish. And the ordinary thugs, whose rifles could kill Matt as dead as any superpower.

Suddenly, approaching Death Metal seemed like a really dumb idea. But Matt was in too far to turn back now. Poising himself to vanish and dodge if he needed to, he willed himself visible.

"I've got this," said Mr. GQ. He raised his hands, and the red light glowed brighter.

"No," Death Metal said. "We really are going to partner up with him."

The handsome man scowled. "You're kidding."

"Strong as we are, he can do things we can't, and we can't afford to pass up any weapon that falls into our hands." Death Metal raised his voice: "Okay, let's get back to the plan! Svergr, figure out which of the wasp ships you want to take. The rest of you, grab alien guns and any other loose gadgets you find. We need to wrap this up and get away."

The others turned toward the crashed vehicles, although in the case of Pretty Boy, not without a final glower.

Matt guessed it was his move again, in a game that felt a lot like chicken. He stepped out from behind Death Metal and, instead of holding Dr. Umbra's pistol on him, let it dangle at the end of his arm.

"I take it," he said, "that capturing a flyer was the point of the fight."

"Of course," Death Metal replied. "Svergr will figure out the wasps' tech, and then we can use it against them."

"How are you going to move the thing? Do you have a truck?"

Death Metal smiled. "Better. A drone that will pick it up and fly it to—"

Matt caught a whispering sound at his back. He turned, and a flying, spinning scrap of fender from a smashed car bashed him in the head.

Pain ripped through his skull, and he staggered. The chunk of steel stopped in mid-air and whizzed at him again. He just managed to lurch out of the way.

He raised his pistol, willed himself to disappear, and then glimpsed a flash from the corner of his eye. He pivoted. Swords whirling like batons–or buzz saws–the kung fu fighter was nearly on top of him.

Matt dodged, and the swordsman came right after him. The villain presumably couldn't see an invisible man, but something, his instincts, training, or a combination of the two, enabled him to guess where Matt had gone.

Matt fired. He didn't *want* to blow the swordsman apart but also didn't know what else to do.

Somehow, the criminal knew the shot was coming. He twisted aside, and the bolt of force shattered a store window across the street.

The kung fu fighter slashed at Matt's head. He ducked, and only realized the attack had been a feint when the real one, a roundhouse kick, slammed into his side.

Stumbling, he tried to shake off the new pain, to scramble back from the swordsman's blades and feet and re-aim the pistol. But before he could, the scrap of fender leaped and once again hit him in the head.

He fell. The kung fu fighter dropped on top of him, groped around for an instant, found his arm, and twisted the pistol out of his grasp. Then he slipped his hands under the bottom of Dr. Umbra's mask so he could dig his fingers into bare neck.

Matt tried to struggle, but it just wasn't happening. He thought, *Invisibility is a shitty power,* and then everything went black.

*

Clarence's power had twisted the steel framework supporting a basketball hoop and acrylic backboard into restraints for hanging a man by his hands. Antoinette Malet, AKA Sweet Lady Q, looked at the prisoner, stripped to his briefs, lean and nice-looking in an ordinary sort of way, and murmured, "I never dreamed he was so young."

"I expected more scars," Clarence replied.

Jeremy grinned a grin that made his flawless face look nasty. "If you want him uglied up…"

"Patience," Clarence said, and then Dr. Umbra groaned. "Aha. He's awake. Welcome back, Doctor."

The superhero blinked, looked around the middle-school gym, then tried to speak. The first time, nothing came out. He swallowed twice and then rasped, "You were just stringing me along until I stopped pointing the gun at you."

"I had to. You caught me without armor, and I know what your pistols can do."

"I thought we had a deal."

Clarence smiled. "I know, and it amazes me. After all the times you've ruined our plans and even put us in jail! Apparently, the wasps have you so feeling so desperate that it got in the way of your common sense."

"You may have been setting me up, but what you said was true: You do need me."

"If Svergr's right, what we need is over there." Clarence nodded to the rebar he'd pulled out of the gym floor, then twisted into a freestanding stick figure. He'd hung Dr. Umbra's cloak, mask, hat, and gloves on it to make a murky thing like the shadow of a scarecrow. The finishing touch had been to close the hands around the grips of the pistols.

"None of it will work for you," Dr. Umbra said.

Clarence shrugged. "Even if Svergr can't figure out your equipment, it's still a good idea to get rid of you."

"Why?"

"Well, for one thing, it'll be great for morale. Look at Freakmaker over there. After all the times you've knocked the teeth out of that perfect smile, he can't wait to see you suffer, and the rest of us have our own scores to settle."

"So it's all about payback, even with the whole world in trouble?"

"No, not all. You see, you were only half right about us. We *are* fighting to kill the wasps, but not to bring back the old order. To build a new one, where *we're* in charge, the law is whatever we say it is, and nobody even remembers the word 'superhero.'"

Dr. Umbra took a breath. "I have no problem with that."

That surprised Antoinette and her teammates too, judging from their expressions. Clarence shook his head and said, "You must think I'm an idiot."

"No," the prisoner said. "I'd rather have people like you running the world than alien monsters."

"Interesting," Clarence said. "I half believe you."

"Then let me down and put me to work. Keep my guns until I earn your trust."

Jeremy laughed. "Not a chance!"

"I'm afraid he's right," Clarence said. "I told you two of the reasons you have to die, and actually, there's even a third one."

"What?"

"We've located several groups of survivors and told them that from now on, they take orders from us. Unfortunately, some have turned out to be resistant. I can't allow that, and I'm hoping that if they watch me put their last surviving superhero to a slow, agonizing, degrading death, it will convince them to fall in line."

"That's me," Jeremy said. "I'm the 'slow, agonizing, degrading death.' I'm going to change you over and over again. Before long, you'll be begging for the next zap because you hope that'll be the one that kills you."

"Wait," Dr. Umbra said. "You're talking about rounding up all the survivors you know about and marching them here to watch?"

Clarence gave a nod. "Zhang Sanfeng, Svergr, and most of the rank and file are out collecting them right now."

"You can't do that. The big hive-ship can fly again. It's floating over the city, which means the wasps can monitor things better than before. If you get that many people moving through the streets at once, they'll see it for sure."

Jeremy sneered. "Nice try."

"Well," Clarence said, "he always was inventive. That's why we shouldn't leave him unguarded."

"I'll stay," said Antoinette and Jeremy in unison.

"You," said Clarence, pointing at her. "You won't give in to the temptation to start the torture early." He turned at Jeremy. "You come have a drink with me. We have a lot to celebrate." He put his hand on his teammate's shoulder and steered him toward the door.

Antoinette waited until they were gone. Then she turned on her power, and it lit up her and her white catsuit with its blue lightning-bolt emblem from the inside, adding its glow to that of the battery-powered and kerosene lanterns the common gang members had set around the gym.

Her electrostatic charge let her climb the painted concrete-block wall and out onto the framework supporting the backboard, hoop, and Dr. Umbra like she was an insect. The steel arms groaned and dipped a little under their combined weight, and the vigilante tensed as she came near.

"It's all right," she said, perching above him and unzipping the pouch clipped to her belt. "I have Tylenol-3's and a bottle of water. You probably need them after the beating you took."

"All right," he said.

Reaching down, the twisted metal bouncing beneath her, she put the capsules in his mouth and then held the plastic bottle to his lips. It was an awkward angle, and some of the water dribbled down his chin

"Better?" she asked.

"Some. Thanks. But why did you bother?"

"Because of years ago, when I was working for AURA, and they left me to die. You didn't. You risked your life to carry me out of the hot zone."

"Set me free, and we'll be even."

She sighed. "That's what you'd do, not me. Maybe once, but not for a long time." Not since her abduction and all that followed. "The best I can do is cut the torture short by killing you myself. I'll say I thought you were starting to turn ghostly and escape."

"Listen to me," he said. "Everything I said is true. I am willing to work with the WMDs, and the wasps are going to notice all those people converging on this location. They'll either pick the groups off on the street or wait for them to get here and hit them all at once. Either way, it's going to be bad."

"We already killed some bugs tonight. We can kill more if we have to."

"You won that fight because you were only fighting a few of them. Since they took the city, they've been stingy about sending out their troops in force. I don't know why. But you can't count on them to react the same way if you give them the chance to kill dozens of people all at once."

Antoinette frowned because what Dr. Umbra was saying sounded plausible...but then, it would, wouldn't it? Like Clarence said, he was "inventive."

Even if what the vigilante claimed was true, she couldn't risk angering and losing her teammates. Not now. Clarence might be happy the wasps had come, but seeing the world in ruins terrified her.

She'd intended to talk with Dr. Umbra for a while and take his mind off what was to come. But she wasn't helping him. He was depressing her. She patted his cheek, then climbed back down the wall.

*

The Tylenol helped but was no match for the pounding Matt had taken, the unyielding tightness of the coils of metal around his wrists, and gravity. He ached from the ends of his arms all way down to the base of his spine, and the pain grew more intense as the minutes crept by.

But it was no worse than the fear that gnawed at him right along with it.

Naturally, he was afraid for himself. He might even be terrified if his experiences since the invasion hadn't toughened him up, and if death by transformation didn't sound so weird, like something out of a fairy tale.

But he was afraid for other people, too. For the survivors the WMDs were forcing out into the open. For Sally and the other friends who depended on him. Thanks to his desperate need to find allies, any allies, he'd let them all down.

He'd even let Dr. Umbra down. The last story anybody would ever hear about the vigilante would be that he'd made a moronic decision, let his enemies catch him, and died screaming and begging like a punk, because Matt doubted he had it in him to die like a hero.

Damn it, he couldn't let himself die, period! He had to find a way out of this.

He surreptitiously studied Sweet Lady Q. Seemingly lost in her own thoughts, she was sitting on the bottom tier of the bleachers several yards away, as if to discourage further conversation.

He could talk to her anyway. He just had to raise his voice. But what could he say that he hadn't tried already?

The only thing he could think of was that he wasn't the real Dr. Umbra, and that seemed like another stupid idea. Sweet Lady Q probably wouldn't believe him, and what if she did? She felt a little bit grateful to the actual hero; she didn't care anything about Matt Brown.

He looked down at the man-shaped frame draped with Dr. Umbra's costume. Presumably, it was there to prove his identity to the WMDs' captive audience, since without it, Matt just looked like any other guy.

He curled his fingers and thought, *Gun.*

Nothing happened. He tried several more times with the same lack of results.

It was no surprise. He wasn't wearing the cloak or the gloves, and the pistols weren't in their holsters. He could think of half a dozen reasons for the trick not to work, but understanding didn't make it any less disappointing.

"Solomon!" he whispered. "Can you hear me? I really, really need your help."

The computer didn't answer. No surprise there, either, but Matt still started to pant and had to struggle to control his breathing.

Think!

The backboard-and-rim assembly kept bouncing minutely and creaking from time to time. What if Death Metal had weakened it when he'd twisted it? What if Matt's weight, and Sweet Lady Q's, when she climbed up on top of it, had weakened it some more?

Heedless of the way it hurt his already tortured arms, Matt swung and kicked back and forth. The makeshift manacles made a louder rasping sound, bounced harder...and stayed in one piece.

Sweet Lady Q looked up, frowned, and stretched out her arm. Matt's muscles clenched in anticipation of a shock. But the bright, crackling bolt stabbed under his feet to blast away a patch of floorboards near the hole Death Metal had already made.

"Stop it," the glowing woman said, sparks crawling in her short, spiky hair. "Even if you could make yourself fall, I'd just tase you."

Matt sighed. "Maybe so. But I had to try something."

She smiled a sad little smile. "I know. But just say goodbye to people in your thoughts, or pray, or whatever feels right. This will all be over soon."

Apparently so; not long after, the thugs started herding frightened people into the gym and onto the bleachers, ordering them to "fill in" and "slide over" like every teacher Matt remembered trying to get a pep rally underway or a class photo taken.

Meanwhile, Matt swung himself, but only slightly, so slightly, he hoped, that neither Sweet Lady Q nor anyone else would notice. He also hoped that even that little bit of motion would weaken his restraints. He couldn't actually tell if it was and doubted it would really help him even if he managed to break them, but trying was better than giving up.

The guy in the junkyard armor–apparently, his name was Svergr–came back in with the survivors he'd collected, and then the kung fu swordsman–Zhang Sanfeng–did the same. Freakmaker entered next, grinning and waving to the crowd like he was some celebrity they were thrilled to see. Then it was Death Metal's turn to swagger in. The gold, silver, and copper of his costume gleamed in the lantern light.

This is it, Matt thought. A bolt of fear stabbed through him, and he strained to keep it from showing in his face.

Death Metal faced the bleachers, and, taking his time about it, looked the audience over. People flinched from his regard.

Finally, the villain said, "As I've explained, my job is to protect you. The last thing I want is to put you through anything unpleasant. But sometimes it's necessary to make an example.

"The man hanging from his hands is the famous Dr. Umbra," Death Metal continued. "There's his costume on the rack. Some of you expected him, or those like him, to swoop in out of nowhere and overturn my authority. *But that is never going to happen.* All the other 'heroes' are dead, and Freakmaker is about to send this one to join his friends."

"Wait," Svergr said.

Death Metal scowled and pivoted to face him. "What?"

"The remote sensors are picking up something," Svergr said. "Moving fast." He paused. "I think we just lost Picket Number Three."

I warned you, Matt thought.

A blast jolted the building. People in the bleachers screamed. The backboard-and-rim assembly bounced, squealed...and held.

"Battle stations!" Death Metal snapped. He whirled back to face the audience. "You people, stay put!"

Patches of the floor burst upward. Pieces of rebar jerked up into view and exploded into dust, which then streamed to Death Metal and coated his body. In a moment, he was the living statue Matt had seen on video. When the change was complete, he strode toward one of the exits.

"Wait!" Matt shouted. "Let me help!"

The gang leader didn't even glance back.

Matt looked around and found Sweet Lady Q, who was glowing and hurrying for a different door. "Lady! Please!"

She *did* look back, and her mouth tightened with something that might have been regret. But then she rushed onward.

In another moment, all the WMDs were gone except for one rifleman staying behind to guard Matt and the audience. More booms shook the building. The attackers buzzed, guns clattered, and men screamed. But the gym was a windowless box, and there was no way to tell who was winning the fight.

Not until Sweet Lady Q scrambled back into the room, headed straight for Matt, and then hesitated. "If I blast it apart, I'll electrocute you," she said.

A section of wall smashed inward, Matt's restraints assembly bounced, groaned, and held, and something as big as a garbage truck crawled through the new hole from the parking lot outside. The intruder was a kind of alien fighter Matt hadn't seen before, and he couldn't tell if it was alive or a machine. It had a dark segmented body studded with metal plates, serrated mandibles projecting from the head, and looked more like a centipede than anything else.

Sweet Lady Q whirled and threw a crackling blast of electricity right between its bulging faceted eyes. The centipede faltered and shuddered, and, yelling like a crazy man, the other WMD blasted it with automatic fire. A ricochet whined past Matt's head.

Then the centipede's eyes glowed blue. Beams like searchlights flared out and caught both the supervillain and the ordinary criminal. They dropped, Sweet Lady Q's internal radiance winking out as she hit the floor.

The centipede scuttled over her, hiding her with its bulk for a moment, and when it crawled on, she was gone. It pivoted toward the bleachers.

Though scared of attracting the centipede's attention, Matt lashed his body back and forth as hard as he could. *Come on, you piece of junk. Break! Break! Break!*

It did. He plummeted and slammed down on the floor.

Meanwhile, screaming people tried to scramble and jump off the bleachers and bolt for the exits. Some of the ones on the ends looked like they might make it. The rest were packed in too tight and shoving and climbing over one another in panic.

The blue beams stabbed up the tiers, and everyone they touched collapsed. Evidently realizing he'd never get off the end of the bleachers in time, a man darted straight forward. He then veered to avoid the centipede, but the thing lurched forward and snapped its mandibles shut around his waist. The man's top half toppled away from the rest of him.

Matt shook off the shock of the fall, tried to stand, and found weight dragging at the ends of his arms. The steel assembly had broken between him and the wall. His wrists were still looped together and tethered to the backboard and rim.

Snarling, he floundered to his feet anyway and hobbled toward the rebar stick figure and Dr. Umbra's gear. He heaved his hands to shoulder level, where Death Metal had positioned the scarecrow's guns.

As he reached for the nearer one, Matt had the sudden horrible conviction that the stick man's grip would be too tight for him to pull the weapon free. It wasn't, though. The pistol slipped out easily.

Unfortunately, Matt couldn't aim it where he needed to. The angle was as awkward as it could be, and his hands were numb and dead.

He staggered to intercept a woman in a hijab who was just jumping off the bleachers. He hitched back and forth to keep her from dodging around him and scurrying on to the exit.

"Take the gun!" he yelled. "Take the gun! Shoot the metal apart!"

After a second, she seemed to understand, but she hesitated. "I don't know—"

"Just press it between my hands and pull the trigger!"

She took the pistol and positioned it where he'd told her. He tensed; for all he knew, she was about to blow his hands off.

Metal clanged, and the backboard banged against the floor. Matt's hands flopped away from one another, and for an instant, that felt wonderful. Then returning circulation set them on fire.

He fumbled the gun back from the Islamic woman. "Run!" he told her, and she did.

As did he, but back to the scarecrow. The way Death Metal had shaped the stick figure, it was hard to get the cloak off. Matt pulled the garment out of the way and shot the rebar apart at the place where the arms and neck came together. Hating the pains and clumsiness that were slowing him down, he grabbed the other pistol and pulled on the costume. As he jerked the wide-brimmed hat down on his head, he turned and discovered the centipede wheeling in his direction.

He willed himself invisible and leaped aside. Blue light splashed where he'd just been standing.

He shot back. The pulse thumped a dent in the wasp-thing's side and made it falter for a split second, but that was all.

As the fight continued, Matt stayed invisible. He had to. After the abuse his body had taken, he didn't dare flicker in and out of sight dodging the alien's rays. He couldn't trust his agility.

Fortunately, his equipment had recharged itself while it was hanging on the stick man. But he knew the needle was dropping moment by moment.

He had to find a way to win, and fast. If only the centipede hadn't knocked out Sweet Lady Q early on, maybe together—

Sweet Lady Q. Exactly what had happened to her, anyway?

At the start of the invasion, Matt had discovered the wasps were particularly interested in catching superheroes. Had they now collected a supervillain, too? If so, there was only one place Sweet Lady Q could be, and that was inside the centipede's body.

He ran in on its flank and slid underneath it like he was sliding into home.

Above him was a circle defined by a groove in the centipede's shell, a ring he hoped opened and closed, although he couldn't tell how. He pointed Dr. Umbra's pistol at it, winced at the sudden realization that shooting it open might kill Sweet Lady Q, and then fired anyway.

The blast blew the circle into a ragged, seeping opening. Matt scrambled up into a cramped compartment that was part fleshy and part metal, like the exposed works he'd seen on the hiveship. He jumped Dr. Umbra's second pistol into his left hand and blasted away with both weapons at once.

The inside of the centipede wasn't as hard as the outside, and the shots ripped long channels through the core. The alien fighter shook hard enough to rattle Matt's bones and then stopped moving.

Matt reappeared, jumped the pistols back into his coat, and turned to Sweet Lady Q. He hadn't hurt her, although the shot that smashed open the circle couldn't have missed her by much. She lay unconscious with strands of the centipede's substance wrapped around her. He suspected they'd reached out like tentacles to pick her up and haul her inside.

Fortunately, it wasn't too hard to pull them loose. He dragged her out of the hole and a few feet away from the centipede.

That's that, he thought. *It's time to get out of here.*

Except that it wasn't, because destroying this one alien fighter wouldn't necessarily be enough to save all the people now sprawled unconscious in the bleachers and on the floor. If the WMDs lost the fight, the wasps would still take everybody prisoner.

"Damn it, anyway," Matt growled. He teleported the pistols back into his hands—even though he hadn't practiced shooting both at once, the centipedes were big enough that they should be hard to miss—and stalked out of the gym and through the locker-lined hallways of the school. Blasts echoed, rattled the fluorescent light fixtures, and made a tube fall out to smash against the linoleum floor. Somewhere, someone kept screaming, "My arms! My arms!" Rising and falling but never stopping, the aliens' buzzing whined like a dentist's drill. The air stank of gun smoke.

It was hellish, but, fear and desperation aside, Matt realized he felt okay. His circulation had come back, exercise had worked the stiffness out of his muscles, and, probably, adrenaline was masking the pain of his bruises. It wasn't much, but it was something.

He rounded a corner and spotted another centipede up ahead. He turned invisible and ran forward.

The thing had smashed through the school's main entrance, and, pivoting and lunging, smashing trophy cases and brushing bulletin boards off the walls, it was trying to catch Zhang Sanfeng in its mandibles. The supervillain slashed at it in return but only scratched it. Rifles banged, although Matt couldn't see the WMDs who were shooting. The centipede's bulk blocked his view of them.

Trying to get onto the alien fighter's back, Zhang leaped high into the air. But, perhaps accidentally, the centipede spun, and then Matt learned that once in a while, even insanely acrobatic superpeople didn't stick the landing. The swordsman fell past his opponent's flank and crunched down amid all the broken glass on the floor. The centipede lifted two of its legs to stamp on him.

Matt fired both pistols. The pulses rocked the alien fighter and gave Zhang a chance to scramble out from under its feet. The centipede pivoted in Matt's direction. Blue light glimmered in its eyes.

Matt dodged toward the lockers on his left, then realized that might not be good enough. The broad rays from the centipede's eyes would pretty much fill the hallway. He threw himself down on his belly, and the blue flashes blazed over his head.

Zhang had gone back to cutting at their enormous opponent's side. "There's a soft spot underneath!" Matt shouted. "Look for a circle!"

The swordsman dived under the centipede, and Matt belatedly wondered if blades would penetrate like a shot from Dr. Umbra's gun. Then Zhang bellowed and stabbed with both his weapons at the same time. The alien fighter faltered, and the villain lunged up inside its body, where, judging from the way it thrashed and heaved, he went on cutting.

The centipede shuddered in a final spasm and froze. Swords now tucked in his sash, Zhang dropped and swung himself clear of it. "WMDs," he said, apparently using some sort of hidden radio, "the walkers have a weak spot on their bellies. Repeat: the walkers have a weak spot on their bellies."

"'Walkers?'" asked Matt, reappearing.

Zhang flashed a grin, and Matt realized with surprise that the villain was a teenager. "Like in *Empire*. It works. Everything else is flying."

"'Everything' meaning what? What all did the wasps throw at us?"

"Besides these things, just the usual. As far as I know."

"Can you and your team handle the walkers now?"

"Death Metal and I can. He's fighting them, too."

"Then I imagine Svergr's in charge of knocking down the flyers. Where's he?"

Zhang pointed with his sword, and Matt ran in the indicated direction.

Svergr had set up shop in what had been the school library. A dozen computer monitors showed swooping, ever-changing views of the area surrounding the school. The images had crosshairs in the centers and words and numbers flickering across the bottoms.

Matt surmised that each monitor was showing the orientation and status of an automated gun, but Svergr wasn't paying any attention to them. Instead, he was working on a weapon like a bazooka on steroids. The whirring, spinning screwdriver he was using for the purpose had apparently slid out of a concealed housing in the index finger of his gauntlet.

"Tell me what's happening," Matt said.

Startled, Svergr took a moment to reply. Then: "These flyers maneuver better than the ones we fought before. But when I get the Bear Killer modified–"

A blast shook the building.

"We may not have enough time," Matt said. "What if I distract the wasps? Would that make them easier to hit?"

"Maybe. Right now, my guns are the only things they have to worry about."

"Then be ready." Matt started to turn away, then realized Svergr hadn't moved. "Do you need to go to a control console or something?"

The armored man snorted. "It's called WiFi, Umbra. I can operate everything just fine from here."

Matt ran on until he found an exit. He took a breath, then scrambled out into a grassy area with bushes and redwood picnic tables.

He shot at the droning, flitting shapes overhead. Vanished. Dodged. Reappeared and started the sequence again, while a blue ray flashed down and smashed a bench to splinters. He tried not to think about the fact that this was exactly how Dr. Umbra had lost his life.

But the vigilante hadn't had Svergr's automated artillery fighting on his side. Or Death Metal, when the WMDs' leader started heaving cars into the air like a catapult. Or Freakmaker shooting his red light from somewhere to maim and cripple individual wasps.

Together, the four of them were enough. Flyers crashed and thudded to the ground until Matt looked around and realized none were left.

*

Peering through a shattered window, Clarence could just barely see Dr. Umbra standing in the smoking, rubble-filled remains of the yard. It really was uncanny how that costume blended with the dark.

Fortunately, though, just barely seeing the vigilante was good enough. The battle had left Clarence exhausted, but Dr. Umbra presumably felt the same way. That meant his guard was down, and if the WMDs struck immediately, they could still dispose of him. It wouldn't be the public spectacle Clarence had wanted, but it would be a whole lot better than nothing.

He touched his collar and activated his com-link. "Svergr, train all your guns on Dr. Umbra. Don't let him see you doing it."

White light gleamed against the wall. "No!" said Sweet Lady Q, her voice coming from right behind Clarence and over the com-link at the same time.

He turned and frowned at her. "Nothing's changed," he said.

"How can you say that? He told us we needed him, and we did. He said he'd fight on our side, and he did that, too."

"It doesn't matter."

"I think it does. What does everybody else think?"

Freakmaker spoke instantly: "Kill him."

"I don't know," said Zhang, his youthful voice troubled. "After what just happened, just shoot him in the back?"

"I've got him," Svergr said. "I'll take the shot if you say so. But, Boss, you might want to think about it. You're not the one watching the feeds, so you maybe don't realize, but the wasps just killed half your soldiers."

Antoinette smiled. "That makes it three to two."

Did she think Clarence had called for a *vote?* He shivered, took a breath to start shouting at her, and then reconsidered.

He was the leader, but the others, the *real* WMDs, were *übermenschen,* too. He had to take their opinions into consideration at least some of the time. Otherwise, they'd rebel, and he couldn't afford that. Not in the middle of a war.

Hell, they might even be right. Maybe Dr. Umbra could be useful, and Clarence could still kill him later. With him hanging around, it would actually be easy.

"Doctor!" he called through the window. "Please don't run off. I'd like to talk more about that partnership you suggested."

The Trade

Flashlight beams shifted back and forth in the darkness, and then, one by one, the WMDs called out from the various aisles.

"No bugs!"

"Okay here!"

"All clear!"

"All right," said Freakmaker, "let's do it."

One of the gang members whooped, and then Matt heard everybody scurrying toward the rear of the Walgreens. The WMDs had a long list of supplies to grab, but apparently no one wanted to miss out on a chance at the controlled substances.

Matt's mouth tightened under his mask. He'd gotten used to looting with Sally and the survivors she led, but this felt different. The WMDs were *rejoicing* in a chance to steal. He turned in a swirl of cloak and headed back outside to wait with the trucks.

Where, immaculately groomed and dressed like a Mafia don in a movie, Freakmaker joined him a few moments later. Matt decided the supervillain must have been keeping a close eye on him. Otherwise, he wouldn't have noticed the ghostly form of "Dr. Umbra" slipping away through the gloom.

"Something bothering you?" Freakmaker asked. His voice had a sneer in it, like he wanted to pick a fight.

"Someone needs to watch for wasps," Matt answered, wondering again what the real Dr. Umbra had done to make the villain hold such a grudge. The mask turned his voice into the usual creepy whisper.

"Are you sure the great superhero isn't having second thoughts about teaming up with a band of evil criminals?"

"Go back inside, Trask. Keep the other 'evil criminals' on task—and out of the Vicodin and Oxycontin—so we can get this done."

"Whatever you say, hero." Freakmaker turned away and then grunted. "Okay, who's this?"

When Matt looked where the supervillain was looking, he spotted a figure half a block away. Then Dr. Umbra's long-distance vision kicked in, and she became a slender college-age girl with short blond hair, glasses, a denim jacket, and jeans. Cute in a nerdy kind of a way underneath the dirt and the air of paranoid wariness every survivor felt out in the open. Despite that watchfulness, she hadn't yet spotted the two men studying her.

"Well?" Freakmaker said. "You can see better than I can."

"It's a girl," Matt said. "Taping up flyers or something."

"Really." Freakmaker slipped his hand in his pocket and ambled in her direction. Concerned about the criminal's intentions, Matt followed along behind.

The girl spotted Freakmaker when she turned away from the wall. She tensed but didn't run. Because he was human, not a wasp, and at first, she probably couldn't see him clearly in the dark. But when he came closer, she gasped.

"I guess you recognize me," Freakmaker said, grinning. He pulled his hand out of his pocket and aimed it at her. Red light throbbed on his fingertips.

"Don't hurt her!" said Matt. The girl jumped again and jerked around in his direction. She'd seen Freakmaker coming, but until this moment, she hadn't spotted him.

"I won't," Freakmaker said. "Not unless she tries to run."

When they reached the girl, he stretched out his hand a little farther. She shuddered, and he laughed. "I just want one of your papers," he said.

She gave him one from the satchel slung over her shoulder. He held it close to his face so he could make out at least some of the hand-written words in the dark. When he finished skimming, he said. "How would you like to take a ride?"

Matt wanted to tell Freakmaker that he couldn't just force her to go with them. But he didn't. Because he couldn't stay partners with the WMDs if he objected to every high-handed or selfish thing they did.

I'll help you if you really need it, he silently promised the girl.

Freakmaker gestured in the direction of the drugstore and the trucks. "Let's go."

*

The broad-shouldered, middle-aged man behind the desk wasn't presently covered in metal, but Gwen Porter still recognized him from the gold panel shirt that gleamed in the candlelight. She almost wished she didn't. It made her situation even scarier, if that was possible.

Death Metal–or Clarence Harvey; Gwen had memorized all the public IDs–took his time reading the two pages that comprised the current edition of *News and Warnings*. Then he looked up at her and smiled.

"I was familiar with many of the journalists in Jackson City," he said. "But I don't recognize you."

She took a breath. Her voice came out shaky anyway. "I was majoring in journalism. I hadn't graduated yet. I had a blog."

"And now, so far as I know, you're the only news source left in town. That's quite a step up. How do you manage it?"

"I just sneak around and watch what's going on. And talk to people. Then I make the flyers and put them up."

Death Metal nodded. "I must say, I respect your courage and dedication, and you've done me a service by reporting one piece of information in particular. But here's the problem. My friends and I are now the government hereabouts, and you've been doing what you do without our authorization."

"Why do you care?" Dr. Umbra whispered. "All she's doing is helping people avoid danger and find supplies."

"If she'd only reported on the wasps and the Greenclaws killings," Death Metal replied, "I might agree with you. But did you notice this?" He put his fingertip on the lower portion of the second page. "She also told people that Svergr visited the auto-salvage yard on Hill Street."

"Well," Gwen said, "he did. Didn't he?"

"Yes," Death Metal said, "but that isn't the point. Your story implies that a WMD is a menace to be avoided no less than a monster in the river or the invaders."

Gwen didn't know how to respond. Fortunately, Death Metal didn't really seem to want an answer. He continued on with barely a pause:

"You need to let go of the past, Ms. Porter. Concepts like crime and supervillainy are obsolete. These days, it's just Earth against the aliens. Dr. Umbra understands. That's why he joined forces with us, isn't it, Doctor?"

"Yes," the vigilante said. He didn't sound especially happy about it, but then again, when everything came out in that sinister whisper, how could anyone tell for sure?

"So you see," Death Metal continued, "you shouldn't encourage people to run away from us. You should urge them to run *to* us. We're the ones with the power to protect them."

Gwen nodded. Too vigorously, maybe. It was hard to keep her movements natural with fear clawing at her nerves. "I understand. I won't write anything about you anymore. Not without asking you first." She hesitated. "Can I go?"

"No," said Death Metal, and then smiled at whatever it was that he saw in her face. "Please, relax. You're not in trouble. But if you left, we'd both be wasting an opportunity."

She swallowed. "What do you mean?"

"I don't know where you've been staying, but I guarantee you this place is safer and more comfortable. You'll be safer, too, with bodyguards to escort you when you venture out into the city. And if that's not enough to convince you, Svergr will provide you with a laptop and printer. As I understand it, he even has plans for radio."

"What do I have to do in return?"

Death Metal's smile widened. "Just what you have been doing, except with some editorial supervision. So you can help our fellow survivors even better than before."

Freakmaker snorted. "I don't see the point of this."

Death Metal shook his head. "That's because you haven't fully freed yourself from the old paradigms, either. As the ruling elite, we need our Dr. Goebbels." His deep-set gray eyes shifted back to Gwen. "Do we have an understanding?"

"Yes," she said. Because what else *could* she say?

*

Matt peered in the doorway. Gwen was staring at the screen of her new laptop but not presently typing anything.

She didn't notice him checking on her, and he didn't speak. Because what would he have said, *Sorry for not saving you?*

Angry with himself for feeling cowardly and ashamed, he turned away. Nobody was mistreating Gwen. She was living in luxury compare to some of the people the WMDs had drafted to work for them. So it was time to forget about her and focus on things he might actually be able to do something about. He climbed back down the stairs to the ground floor, tugged his slouch hat down on his head, and stepped outside.

After the wasps attacked the middle school, the WMDs had relocated to a row of townhouses on an otherwise uninhabited residential street. The broken doors, shattered windows, and charred marks on exterior and interior walls revealed that at some point, the aliens had made a sweep through the neighborhood. Bloated, stinking corpses had told the same story before Death Metal ordered them cleared away.

The trucks and vans were idling at the curb. Sweet Lady Q–Antoinette–was riding in the back of the lead pickup. She smiled and waved when she saw Matt approaching.

He climbed up beside her. It was their job to watch for aliens flying overhead and shoot them down if necessary.

He settled himself, and then, managing without headlights, the convoy set off through the dark, ravaged streets. And as they left the townhouses behind, he started to feel a little better.

Because this was the answer to everything that was weighing on his conscience. He'd teamed up with the WMDs to protect people.

Tonight's foray wouldn't be as satisfying as a raid on the wasps, but it still mattered. The Greenclaws monster, if a monster was what it really was–as was so often the case, he wished he'd paid more attention to news about superheroes and their enemies–was slaughtering foragers who wandered too close to the river. Death Metal meant to put a stop to that, and if it helped him convince people he and his gang had turned into the good guys, Matt supposed that was a small price to pay to save lives.

"It's a nice night," said Antoinette.

The comment seemed crazy, but he realized that if a person could ignore the shattered skyline and the dead bodies in the streets, she had a point. The air was pleasantly cool, and the sky was clear and full of stars. "I suppose," he replied.

"You fought Greenclaws," she said. "What's he–or it–like?"

He tried to come up with an answer that wouldn't give him away: "Honestly, I never got that close. Red Bear and Magnetar finished him off."

She cocked her head. "But you, like, studied him, right? Because you always learned everything you could about all us villains."

"Well," Matt said, "that was what I wanted everyone to think. But sometimes I was just too busy."

She laughed. "Don't worry. Your secret's safe with me."

A few minutes later, the convoy rolled to a stop in the parking lot beside a warehouse. The black surface of the river showed through the gap between that building and the next one, and the smell of the water hung in the air.

Matt jumped out of the pickup, took another look at the sky, and listened for buzzing, too. As far as he could tell, there were no wasps around. There was no sign of Greenclaws, either.

Two of the plates that armored Svergr's forearm slid apart. Half a dozen drone cameras the size of pistachios floated out of a little compartment and up into the air, then shot off in the direction of the river.

After that, everyone stood around and waited. Until eventually, the rogue scientist in his bulky, lopsided armor said, "I'm not seeing anything. Of course, Greenclaws could be underwater."

"Or just lying low," Freakmaker said. "Why don't we send in the superhero to scout on the ground?" He leered at Matt. "This *is* your kind of job, right? The reason we keep you around?"

Matt took a breath and then said, "Fine." Because he was sure the real Dr. Umbra would have agreed, so he had no choice but to do the same. He jumped a pistol into his hand and headed for the shadowy alleyway between the buildings.

In the tense half hour that followed, he decided it was no surprise Svergr's drones hadn't found anything. Together, the cavernous warehouses, sheds, cranes, forklifts, docks, and moored barges made a maze where almost anything could hide. And pounce out at the guy stupid enough to come looking for it.

But to Matt's relief, that wasn't the way he finally found his quarry. He stepped out of the maintenance and office building he'd just finished exploring, turned left, and spotted a hunched shape crouching at the water's edge. The sight made his stomach turn over.

Not because the somewhat manlike creature was ugly, although, with its scales, frills of fin, round black eyes, hooked claws, and jaws like an alligator gar, it definitely was. The wasps were even worse in that regard. No, the really sickening thing was the way the monster–Greenclaws–was squatting beside a dead person, ripping away handfuls of rotting flesh, and stuffing them in its mouth.

Matt slipped his finger under the collar of his caped coat and touched the button Svergr had given him. "I see him," he whispered. "Get a fix on my location."

"Got it," the inventor replied.

"Then move in *quietly*. The thing's right beside the river. If it hears you coming, all it has to do is dive in."

Death Metal's voice came over the com: "Understood. I'm leaving the riflemen with the trucks, but we supers are on our way."

No doubt they were, but unfortunately, Greenclaws decided to move before they showed up. Rising from the shredded, emptied-out husk of its meal, the monster turned toward the water.

Matt fired.

The burst of force knocked Greenclaws down but didn't tear it apart like it would a wasp. The creature scrambled to its feet, cast about, and then, spotting Matt despite his shadowy camouflage, snarled and rushed him.

Matt backpedaled and kept shooting. Sometimes he knocked Greenclaws down again and bloodied the creature as well. But sometimes he missed, or the monster dodged, and shambling stride by shambling stride, it was closing the distance.

Matt wanted to go invisible but feared Greenclaws might run away if it couldn't see its attacker anymore. So he delayed switching on the power for another instant, and then another after that.

Until a bright, crackling bolt of electricity burned into Greenclaws's torso, and the monster flailed in a spastic dance. A forklift arced through the air and smashed down on top of it.

Greenclaws heaved itself up and out from under the lifting device. By the time it regained its feet, Zhang Sanfeng was rushing it. The creature raked at the teenager, and he ducked the blow and slashed with his swords at the same time. Doubling over, Greenclaws clutched at the guts spilling out of its belly, and, bellowing, Zhang spun another cut down at the top of its head. The man-eater dropped. Zhang stamp-kicked its neck, and bone snapped.

Matt realized he was panting, and shaking a little too. He struggled to stop doing both before anyone noticed.

The rest of the WMDs gathered in to look at Greenclaws's body. Smirking, Freakmaker took note of how close the creature had come to Matt and said, "What a shame if we'd showed up just a few seconds later."

"We should take the body," Death Metal said, "to prove to any Doubting Thomases we really did kill it. Ms. Porter can run a photo of it in her next edition."

Water splashed. Matt and his companions pivoted toward the sound just in time to see something huge heave itself up onto the concrete walkway beside the river.

It was like the monster they'd just killed but big as a dinosaur. Its jaws could have chewed up a car, and its long legs crossed the several yards that separated it from the humans in just a couple hops.

A hand with webbed fingers and claws as long as Zhang's blades swept down like it was swatting a fly. Matt frantically leaped away, and others did, too. He pointed his pistol. Freakmaker's hands glowed red, and Sweet Lady Q's whole body lit up.

"Don't!" Death Metal gasped. Matt looked and saw that the leader of the WMDs lay pinned under the monster's hand. And since he wasn't armored up, if the creature applied a little more pressure, it would surely squash him flat.

Matt held his fire. So did everyone else.

"Good," the monster growled, water dripping from its fins, the gill slits in its neck opening and closing.

Matt caught his breath. He supposed that after everything he'd already been through, nothing should surprise him anymore. But still, he hadn't expected the creature to speak.

"I take it," Death Metal wheezed, "that you're the *real* Greenclaws. The thing we just fought was only a servant."

"Yes," the creature said. "Spawn many." It turned its head to look at Matt with eyes as big as tires. "Warned you. Grow into Greenclaws that can kill you."

"But you didn't try," Death Metal said. "Why not? What do you want?"

"Bargain," Greenclaws said. It lifted its hand, and, moving cautiously, like he suspected that freeing him was a trick, Death Metal clambered to his feet.

"River and shores mine," the monster continued. "Do what I want. Hunt."

"Yeah, right," said Zhang. He slashed his swords into a guard position, one high, one low.

But Death Metal raised his hand and said, "Hold on. Let's hear him out."

"Why?" Freakmaker asked. "I mean, now that it was stupid enough to let you up."

Because we're all still where it can just reach out and smash us? Matt thought, his pulse beating in the side of his neck. Damn, the thing was big!

"Because he's about to explain what *we* get out of the deal," Death Metal said. "Aren't you, Greenclaws?"

"Tools and things here," the creature said. "Don't need. Humans need."

The enormous energy bazooka called the Bear Killer resting on his shoulder, Svergr looked up at the giant. "Is there metal?" he asked. "Copper? Steel?"

"Yes."

"Good," Freakmaker said. "After you're gone, we'll help ourselves."

"Eat you if you want," Greenclaws said. "But more to trade. Something humans not get without me. Submarine."

Death Metal cocked his head. "All right, that *is* interesting."

"Yes," Greenclaws said. "Wasps watch sky and ground. Submarine go where they don't see."

"Svergr can build a sub," said Zhang. "He can build anything."

"Given time," the scientist said, "sure. Still, if we had one now, I could put it to good use."

"You certainly could," Death Metal said. He looked up at the monster looming over them. "So we agree the river is your sovereign territory, and you let us scavenge here and give us a submarine."

Greenclaws shook its head, and even though he'd already learned the thing could talk, for some reason, that human-like gesture unsettled Matt.

"Give plenty," the river creature growled. "Humans give plenty, too. Or no trade. Fight."

"What else do you want?" Death Metal asked.

"People. Alive people. Show you trustworthy. Show you friends."

Death Metal frowned. "I suppose I could spare a dozen. I'll just need a little time to collect them"

"Full moon soon. Bring then." Greenclaws backed away, whirled, leaped, and plunged into the river. Matt let out his breath, and tension quivered out of his body.

'Well," Death Metal said, "shall we head on back to the trucks?" He glanced down at the carcass of Greenclaws's spawn. "Under the circumstances, we won't be needing that after all."

As they walked down the alleyway between two warehouses, Matt said, "That worked out all right. It would have been risky to fight the creature when we weren't ready. Now that we know what we're really up against, we can make a plan."

Death Metal shook his head. "I'm sorry if it offends your sensibilities, Doctor, but we already have a plan."

Matt stopped and turned to face the other man. Everyone else stopped, too, and it hit him like a splash of ice water that each of them, even Sweet Lady Q, was a murderer who'd tried to kill Dr. Umbra in the past. With an inhuman horror towering over them all, he'd halfway forgotten that, but trapped in this narrow space with them, he was sure as hell remembering now.

And what could he say that would sway a Hitler wannabe like Death Metal? Obviously, not that sending innocent people to their deaths was wrong. He'd probably laugh at that. Matt had to make his arguments *practical*.

"My 'sensibilities' aren't the issue," he said. "We came here for a purpose: to improve the WMDs' reputation."

"We still will," Death Metal said. "By killing more wasps."

"But what about the *negative* PR you'll get from backing down when Greenclaws turned out to be tougher than we thought?"

"Tougher than the rest of us thought," Freakmaker said. "The thing recognized you, and maybe you knew more about it than you told us. Maybe you were hoping it would get the drop on us and kill us."

"Don't be stupid," said Matt, He turned back to Death Metal. "It'll also look bad when you give people to a monster to be eaten."

"But no one outside the organization knows we ever planned to kill Greenclaws," the supervillain replied, "and if we're discrete, hardly anyone will know we ended up handing over a few of our people instead. Remember, we control the news."

"But how can you be a king if you don't have anybody to rule?"

"I'll still have all my useful subjects," Death Metal said. "We'll give Greenclaws the sick and the weak. The shirkers and malcontents. It's what leaders have to do in difficult times: cull the herd."

*

Gwen raised the window. Despite her caution, it squeaked, and she cringed.

But no one called out, and no footsteps came thumping up the stairs on the other side of the bedroom door. Her mouth dry and her heart pounding, she realized it had only been a little noise, not the grating squeal it had sounded like to her.

She peered out at the night. She was only on the second story of the townhouse, but she'd never liked heights, and it looked like a long way to the ground.

No, she insisted to herself, *it isn't. Superheroes, even the ones without powers, jump farther than that all the time.*

She knew because she studied superpeople. She'd hoped to cover them after she graduated. Maybe for Meta, the cable news channel.

But she also knew *she* was no superhero. She was just a normal person who might be about to break her legs or worse.

Doing her best to ignore that demoralizing truth, she clambered out the window feet first. She hung from the sill, then dropped.

The impact jolted her and dumped her on her back in the wet grass. She gasped in a breath, tried to move, and found that she could. She hadn't broken anything after all.

She scrambled up and took another look around. No WMDs were coming. Apparently no one had heard her bump down on the ground, either.

So, run! she thought. *Just get away!*

But she couldn't. Not yet. Not by herself.

She hadn't made any trouble since her capture, and the WMDs had gotten used to having their "Dr. Goebbels" around. They spoke freely on the first floor, where Death Metal had his "command center," without realizing or caring how their voices echoed up the stairs to her room. Which was how she found out they were rounding up people for Greenclaws to kill and eat.

And it was too much. She was no hero or police officer or anything like that. But she couldn't just stand by and let it happen any more than she'd been able to keep hiding inside her bombed-out apartment building once she realized information could mean the difference between life and death to other survivors.

She tiptoed down the strip of grass between Death Metal's townhouse and the one next door and peeked out into the strip of adjacent backyards. Still no bad guys. Of course, they might be looking out windows. Svergr's cameras and motion detectors were certainly keeping watch from rooftops and under the eaves.

But if she hugged the walls as she crept along, maybe she could go undetected.

Sneak like a ninja, she told herself. *Or like Dr. Umbra, not that he'd turned out to be good for anything. There had always been people who claimed he wasn't a real hero, and unfortunately, they'd turned out to be right.*

As she moved, she looked for something to use as a weapon. A fist-sized chunk of an overturned and shattered concrete birdbath caught her eye. She picked it up and clutched it tight.

She'd heard Freakmaker say the prisoners were in the next-to-last townhouse in the row. She double-checked to make sure she had the right one, took a deep breath, and then tapped rapidly on the back door. She wanted it to sound urgent but not be so loud that people in other buildings would hear.

Footsteps bumped on the other side of the door, and she stifled another urge to turn and run. The door opened, and a WMD in urban camouflage fatigues looked out. He was about her own age, with a wispy moustache and tattooing crawling up his neck. When he saw her, his brown eyes widened.

"Wasps," she whispered. "They're here."

"What?" He peered past her into the empty back yard. "I don't hear anything."

"I know," she said. "I don't understand it, either. But I saw them crawling on the roofs and in the trees. You've got to—"

She swung her chuck of concrete at the side of his face.

The impact jolted her arm and him, too, apparently, because he staggered a step. Frantic now, knowing she didn't dare give him a chance to strike back, she hit him again and again.

He grunted and dropped to one knee. She pounded at the black, shiny hair on top of his head. Blood poured from gashes in his scalp, and then he fell over sideways into the wall. He left red streaks on it as he slumped on down to the floor.

Gasping, the raw, scraped inside of her hand stinging, she dropped her piece of concrete and pulled the rifle out of his grip. She'd never shot a gun in her life, but the weapon might deter an attacker or pursuer even if she couldn't hit anything.

She tiptoed on through a small laundry room, kitchen, and breakfast nook, then found the prisoners in the living room. They were all staring right at her. They'd heard the fight and were waiting to see who would show up in the doorway.

"Come with me," she said. "We're running away."

"No," said a skinny, shirtless man with brown-stained linen wrapped around his middle. "They'll punish us."

"They're going to kill you," Gwen replied. "We don't have time for explanations, but I swear it's true. You have to–"

The prisoners' eyes widened. A woman gasped. Gwen realized someone was behind her.

She jerked around. His face a pulpy mess, one eye swollen shut, the gang member she'd attacked was stumbling toward her with a pistol in his hands. God, how had she missed noticing that he had a second gun? How had she not realized he wasn't actually unconscious?

Without her even wanting it–or at least that was how it felt–her finger jerked the trigger of the assault rifle. Nothing happened.

"Safety's on," the WMD slurred. His lips were mashed and split, and two of his teeth were broken. "Don't look for it. Drop the gun *now.*"

She crouched and set the rifle on the floor. Then the front door of the townhouse banged open. She realized the guard must have radioed for reinforcements before coming after her.

"What's this?" Svergr asked. Gwen had never heard him sound especially surprised, excited, or upset, and he didn't now, either. Somehow, his matter-of-fact tone reminded her of her mechanic asking what seemed to be the trouble with her car.

"The writer wanted to help them escape," said the guard.

"From the looks of you, she gave it a pretty good try, too. Go get yourself some first aid. Bob, you're on guard duty here. Miss Porter, you need to come with me."

"She said you're going to kill us," whimpered a morbidly obese female prisoner. "That's not true, is it?"

"Everything's okay," Svergr said, without bothering to turn his helmeted head in her direction. "Come on, Miss Porter."

She doubted he meant to hurt her. During her captivity, she'd never seen him hurt anyone or do much of anything but tinker with his gadgets. But he was going to take her to those who very well might, and so it was hard to make herself cross the room. But she did. Because it was better to cooperate than be manhandled.

Smelling of oil, armor clanking, whirring, and humming, Svergr marched her back to the townhouse from which she'd escaped mere minutes before. Death Metal was waiting behind his desk in the command center. Nearly a parody of masculine beauty and style, like a leading man from Hollywood's golden age, Freakmaker lounged in an easy chair smoking a cigarette and blowing smoke rings. A murky ghost in the candlelight, Dr. Umbra stood beside what little remained of a home entertainment system. Someone–Svergr, no doubt–had torn the plasma TV and other electronics apart.

"Well, young lady," Death Metal said, "I have to say, I'm disappointed. I did everything I could to give you a tolerable life and help you achieve your ambitions, and in return, you stabbed me in the back."

Gwen suspected it would be impossible to talk her way out of this. Still, she had to try. She took a long, steadying breath.

"I didn't *want* to go against you," she said. "I mean, when Freakmaker first brought me here, I was afraid because...well, you know why. But after that, there were times when I thought, well, maybe all this, the forced labor and the rest of it, is just the way things have to be. Maybe I should be grateful to have enough to eat, and superpeople to protect me the next time the wasps come around."

Death Metal shrugged. "I would have said so."

"But you can't just give up people to be slaughtered! That's wrong in any time and any situation. You claim you're our leader and protector now, not just a criminal. If that's even a little bit true, you must see you're doing something bad!"

Death Metal sighed. "I don't know where you acquired such naive ideas, Ms. Porter–television and the movies, I suspect–but here in the real world, leaders send people to their deaths all the time."

"Soldiers, maybe, but this is different!"

"No, not really. In either case, the leader accepts a lesser evil to produce a greater good. Eventually, if we all do what we need to, the wasps will only be a memory, and the human race will control the world once more. When that day comes, will you honestly be able to say this sacrifice wasn't worth it?"

"Yes! Because it really is 'evil!' And besides, you can't know this one decision is going to make some huge difference later on!"

Death Metal frowned. "All right, that's a valid point. I can't *know*, obviously. But I have to make the hard choices as they present themselves and hope the sum total of my efforts produces victory. And unfortunately, the next hard choice is you."

Gwen's mouth went dry.

Freakmaker leered. "I can teach her to behave herself."

Dr. Umbra addressed himself to Death Metal: "Giving her to Trask would be a waste. If he kills or cripples her, she won't be able to do her work."

"The problem," Death Metal said, "is that I no longer trust her to do it in any case. Her perspective and ours are just too different."

Freakmaker's grin widened even further, exposing more of his white, perfect teeth.

"But, Jeremy," Death Metal continued, "I have to say, I *do* agree it would be wasteful to give her to you when Greenclaws is waiting for us to pay him in human lives. One of the lives might as well be Ms. Porter's, and we probably should make sure she still looks and tastes human."

"Shit," Freakmaker said, plainly irritated but trying to cover it with a show of humor, "I never get to have any fun."

Death Metal looked Gwen in the eye. "Perhaps it will comfort you to know your work will continue. Somewhere, I'll find a reporter with the same initiative but a more realistic attitude to take up where you're leaving off."

Gwen spun around toward Dr. Umbra. She'd written him off before, but he was the only hope she had left.

"You're a hero," she said. "*Please* don't let them do this. Not to me or any of the others!"

The inscrutable black eyes peered back out of his otherwise featureless blur of a face. Then he simply said, "I'm sorry."

*

As Matt drove and scanned the sky for wasps, he watched the rearview mirror, too. With the possible exception of Sweet Lady Q, none of the WMDs actually trusted him. Heck, Freakmaker would *love* to catch him doing something underhanded. So it was entirely possible that somebody would try to tail him. But it didn't look like anybody was.

All of which, he reflected as he pulled to a stop in front of the waterfront warehouses, might only mean it would be a river monster that killed him rather than a bug from another planet or a supervillain. This was really going to be dangerous, so much so that if not for his memory of the mingled despair and disgust in Gwen's face when he said he wouldn't help her, he might have decided not to get out of the car.

Even though he knew he didn't *deserve* to feel ashamed. How else could he have answered with Death Metal, Freakmaker, and Svergr all right there in the room? The truth was, he'd *been* trying to help the prisoners all along, at first, by working on Antoinette and Zhang Sanfeng, or, to use his real name, David Lo.

Sweet Lady Q had a soft spot for Matt, the more so now that "Dr. Umbra" had saved her life for a second time. And David was just a teenager surprisingly like many other young athletes Matt had known. The kid was all about the excitement and glory of being the best kung fu fighter in the world and would slice up anybody to test himself or validate his reputation. But otherwise, he didn't come across as mean, and Matt had hoped that if he could get him to stop practicing kata long enough to think about it, he might decide murdering defenseless prisoners violated some Wudang code of honor.

Unfortunately, though, Matt's cautious probing and coaxing hadn't worked on either of them. He got the feeling they didn't especially *like* what their leader planned to do but saw no reason to make a stink about it. Maybe they'd watched or even helped him do so many despicable things in the past that it just wasn't a big deal anymore.

So then Matt had considered doing exactly what Gwen had tried to do, helping the captives run away. With Dr. Umbra's powers, he could probably pull it off, but unfortunately, only if he was willing to run away right along with them. There was no way he could sell the WMDs on the idea that some *other* invisible man had overpowered the guard, and as long as the wasps were in control of Jackson City, giving up superpowered allies just wasn't an option.

So what did that leave? As far as Matt could figure, only the dumb-ass move he was trying now. He jumped a raygun into his hand and prowled toward the river.

How, he wondered, would somebody go about hiding a submarine on a strip of commercial docks and warehouses? The original owners must have kept it parked on top of the water, not underneath. Otherwise, how could they have boarded or disembarked? And if it was floating on the surface, they must have disguised it somehow.

He started around a pile of crates, then heard a kind of soft slap coming from the other side. His imagination instantly supplied an image to account for the sound, a webbed, scaly foot like a scuba fin taking a clumsy, smacking step.

He willed himself invisible a split second before one of Greenclaws's spawn came around the crates. It didn't react, didn't see him, but with its next step, it would blunder right into him.

Matt backpedaled. He just needed a space to duck into while the creature passed on by, but suddenly, there didn't seem to be one. Piles of boxes, an old oil drum pressed into service as a trash can, and a tractor hooked to a string of flatbed carts penned him in like walls.

Afraid of making noise, he nonetheless scrambled up on one of the wagons. The aluminum made a little clanking noise as it took his weight. The spawn, however, lumbered on past without noticing.

His heart thumping, Matt gave the monster a few seconds to shamble farther away. Then he climbed down off the cart and, feeling the usual reluctance when he knew he was still in danger, reappeared.

He dodged two more such creatures over the course of the next couple hours, and caught himself checking his watch more and more often. He wanted to be away from here before dawn. Dr. Umbra's camouflage wouldn't work nearly as well in the daylight.

But he couldn't leave until he found the sub because now was his only shot. Tomorrow was the first night of the full moon.

The *almost*-full one set, and a gray hint of light appeared on the eastern horizon. He shook his head in frustration. He'd only covered a fraction of the docks on this side of the river. And what if the sub was on the other side?

He wondered if the real Dr. Umbra would have done better and decided the answer was almost certainly yes. Supposedly, the vigilante had been a master detective, and Matt had never felt more inadequate by comparison. Even with all the original's gear to prop him up, he was, at his absolute best, only half a hero, a–

A barge caught his eye, or rather, the barge and its mooring in combination. Rust and streaks of filth mottled the boat's steel hull. Trash littered the deck, and spatters of bird shit dotted the fiberglass cargo cover. There was no tugboat tied up anywhere near the vessel, and in general, it looked neglected and forgotten.

Yet there was a sturdy chain-link gate with an electronic lock blocking access to the pier to which it was tied, and a prominent AUTHORIZED PERSONNEL ONLY – TRESPASSERS WILL BE PROSECUTED sign attached to the gate.

Really, the combination didn't look all *that* strange. Still, it was odd enough to get Matt's blood pumping a little faster, maybe just because he was feeling desperate.

He took a look around for wasps, spawn, or Greenclaws itself, then shot the gate open. He winced at the metallic *crack*, but nothing came rushing to investigate.

He strode out onto the dock and then aboard the barge. Still, nothing bothered him. Reminding himself not to drop his guard, he inspected the fiberglass cover. He didn't know anything about barges, but the thing must lift, fold, or open up somehow.

Thanks to his mask's night vision, he found a panel nobody would have noticed from ten feet away, even in the daylight. He experimented and found that it slid to the right. On the other side was a circular shaft with a ladder bolted to the wall.

For all Matt knew, maybe barges were built like this. Maybe this was just a way inside the hull. He hoped, though, that it was a way into a whole different vessel clinging to the underside of the barge.

He climbed down, noting he passed through what appeared to be some sort of open hatch in the process. At the bottom was a long, dark corridor with cramped little nooks and compartments to either side. He didn't know any more about submarines than he did about barges–he was discovering that impersonating a superhero was an excellent way to find out just how many things you didn't know–but the general layout seemed right.

If this was a sub, the control room was presumably at one end or the other. He arbitrarily headed right and after several paces noticed the insignia painted on a locker, an "A" superimposed on a ragged sunburst.

He knew just enough about them to recognize the emblem of AURA, Anarchists United for Radical...something. He wondered if Greenclaws had actually worked with a terrorist organization. It was hard to see why the river monster would bother, but then again, the possibility was no weirder than a lot of other things Matt had run into recently.

It turned out that he'd guessed correctly about where to find the control room. From the movies, he recognized sonar screens and a periscope, but everything had an ultra-high-tech look to it. If Svergr ever got his hands on the sub, his teammates wouldn't be able to pry him away.

But Matt was here to make sure the outlaw scientist never would get his hands on it. If Greenclaws didn't have a working sub to trade, the WMDs would have no reason to hand over Gwen and the other prisoners.

The easiest way to take care of that might be to blast important parts of the vessel to pieces. Matt was reluctant to go that route because, while saving the captives' lives was the most important thing, he also wanted the sub for himself if he could get it, It offered a way to find out what was going on outside the city, and maybe even if his mom, dad, and brother were still alive in Port Barnett a thousand miles away.

He looked around and spotted a swivel chair in front of a particularly impressive-looking array of controls. The pilot's seat, he suspected.

He jumped his pistol back into its holster, sat down, and took a breath. *Go slow,* he told himself. *Look for menus. Or something like an autopilot. That's what you really need.*

But first, he suspected, he needed to turn the whole system on. He looked around and found a button labeled Power. He hesitated for a second and then pressed it.

The console hummed softly. The oval screen glowed blue and then showed the A-and-sunburst emblem, red on a purplish background. Icons popped into view. It was like his iMac booting up, before the wasps had blasted it and his whole apartment complex to rubble, except that turning on his computer to waste time with YouTube or whatever had never brought a whole room or chain of rooms to life.

All the other consoles started glowing and displaying icons or streaming readouts as well. Fluorescent lights came on in the ceiling, and then down the corridor that ran the length of the sub. Vibration shivered through the floor.

Matt grinned. Maybe this wasn't going to be so hard.

Then all the monitors turned black except for a prompt in white letters in the middle: ENTER PASSWORD.

Shit! He found his keyboard and typed in AURA.

The vibration in the floor grew more pronounced, and a droning sounded from astern. The sub was doing something. Something it had been programmed to do when some idiot of an intruder failed to input the right password.

And of course it wasn't AURA. What kind of security would that be? Matt struggled to think of something clever but could only come up with ANARCHIST and ANARCHY, more words too obvious to be correct. He tried them anyway.

And something changed, but unfortunately, not for the better. A gushing, the unmistakable sound of streaming water, drowned out the thrum of the engines.

Matt realized the sub was going to scuttle itself and drown him in the process. He thought with a crazy hilarity that was really a form of terror that it was a cost-cutting way of keeping the vessel out of enemy hands. AURA saved money on things like poison gas and explosives. Maybe they'd even hoped they could recover their property later.

Two names from high-school history class popped into his head. He entered SACCO and then VENZETTI. They didn't work, either.

A sheet of water rippled in from the passage and licked around the soles of his cross-trainers.

He jumped up from his chair, backed away from the row of consoles, and teleported his pistols into his hands. Firing shot after shot, he smashed screens, switches, buttons, and keyboards. Fire flickered, and smoke billowed into the air.

But the gushing noise didn't stop, and water kept pouring into the control room. It was already halfway to his knees.

He jumped the rayguns back into their holsters and waded back down the passage. He needed to get out of the sub wherever the water was coming in. Assuming he could find an opening in time.

The lights went out. Thanks to his mask, that didn't hinder him, but the water did. It reached his waist and then his breastbone. It shoved him backward as it rushed down the length of the sub. He grabbed whatever was in reach to drag himself along against the force of the current. His cloak streamed out behind him.

The first opening he came to was the same hatch through which he'd descended. The river poured down the ladder like a waterfall.

He wasn't sure he could climb up against the force of the torrent, and even with something close to panic gnawing at him, decided not to waste strength trying. Instead, clinging to the edge of an alcove, he floated and breathed the air in the steadily dwindling space above the water.

He all but kissed the ceiling to suck in the very last of it, then swam for the hatch. With the sub completely full of water, there was no pressure to push him back anymore.

But there was still depth to kill him if he let it, because the vessel had dived all the way to the muddy bottom of the river. Kicking, his chest aching, he floundered up a hundred feet—or at least it felt like a hundred—before his head broke water and he gasped in his next breath.

And then he saw there was still distance to contend with. The sub had been able to dive as deep as it had because it had traveled a long way from the docks.

It occurred to Matt that if he wanted to make absolutely sure he reached the shore before his stamina gave out, he'd be smart to drop the caped coat. It was weight, the pistols inside were, too, and, long and voluminous as it was, the garment was likely to hamper the action of his legs.

Yet he couldn't just throw away the source of Dr. Umbra's powers. It was pure dumb luck that he had them in the first place, but he was responsible for them nonetheless.

Treading water, he drew a deep breath and then struck out for the piers. Meanwhile, the current carried him downstream, and he realized that on top of everything else, he was in for a long hike back to his car.

*

The pickup hit a pothole. Or maybe, Antoinette thought, a piece of rubble or a dead body. Either way, the jolt made Dr. Umbra jerk and look around wildly.

She smiled and said, "We just hit a bump. Were you dozing?"

He hesitated and then replied, "Maybe for a second. I didn't get much sleep last night."

"Who does anymore?" Not that she'd ever thought of him as really needing to sleep, let alone expected him to admit that kind of human weakness. He was different than she'd imagined, and she liked him better for it. She hoped that, now that they were getting to know each other in a way that had been impossible before, he felt something similar.

After another couple minutes, the convoy rolled to a stop in the same parking lot as last time. The WMDs climbed out of their various vehicles and herded the prisoners out at gunpoint.

When Antoinette took in the fear manifest in their faces and trembling, balking body language, she felt a little twinge of regret. She'd never liked the hostage-taking part of being a supervillain, especially when it became necessary to hurt them, and she suspected that naturally, this particular situation bothered Dr. Umbra a lot more than it did her.

That was one more reason to get it over with. Then they could put it behind them.

Clarence definitely looked eager to get it done. "Let's go," he said, and everyone headed toward the water with the round white eye that was the full moon looking down from overhead.

At first, as they prowled around, the docks seemed deserted, and Antoinette wondered if Greenclaws had forgotten all about the deal. Because after all, who knew how smart the monster really was or how its mind worked? But after a while, Dr. Umbra pointed and whispered, "Over there."

She looked and saw one of the spawn keeping pace with their little band of supers, riflemen, and prisoners. And not long after that, water splashed, and Greenclaws heaved itself up onto the walkway from which the various docks extended.

Antoinette clamped down on the impulse to turn on her power. If everything went okay, she wouldn't need it, and she didn't want to glow if she didn't have to. The wasps might see.

Greenclaws looked at the humans, and then its belly rumbled. There was something shockingly, gruesomely funny about that, but not to the captives. They gasped, yelped, and cowered. One man turned to run, but he found himself staring down the muzzle of an AK-47, and that was the end of that.

"You bring," Greenclaws said. "Good. Give."

"First, show us the sub," Dr. Umbra said. It surprised Antoinette a little. He generally let Clarence do the talking, especially when the gang was doing something a superhero wouldn't approve of.

"Yes," Death Metal said. "*Then* we'll make the exchange."

Greenclaws peered back at them for a moment. Then it grunted and said, "Come." It turned and shuffled down the walkway, brushing over a stack of pallets as it passed. The humans followed. A couple prisoners started begging for their lives.

Dr. Umbra nodded to the left. "There's another spawn shadowing us."

"Yeah," said Zhang, fingering the tasseled hilt of the sword on his right hip, "I spotted it, too."

Greenclaws stopped in front of a dock with a grubby old barge tied up beside it. The monster tore away the chain-link gate intended to limit access with a casual sweep of its talons.

"Submarine under raft," Greenclaws said. "Go. Look."

The supers all hesitated, and Antoinette realized that, powers notwithstanding, everyone felt the same reluctance to split off from the group and walk right up to the monster. But then Svergr muttered, "Screw it," shifted his grip on the Bear Killer, and did exactly that.

Greenclaws let him pass by unharmed and head out onto the pier. The planks creaked under the weight of his clicking, whirring armor. He climbed onto the barge, and, after a little investigation, found a sliding panel in the fiberglass cargo cover. He leaned forward and looked inside.

"Well?" Clarence called.

"Tell you in a second," Svergr answered. He was trying to sound like nothing was wrong, but Antoinette could hear the sudden tension in his voice.

And apparently Greenclaws could, too. The creature planted itself right at the end of the dock, blocking the way off. "Tell *now,*" it growled.

"Fine," Clarence rapped, now sounding reasonably menacing in his own right. "Boss, at one time, there may have been something hanging under the barge. But it's not there anymore."

"Liar!" Greenclaws snarled.

"You're the liar," Dr. Umbra said. "You tried to con us."

"No lie," the monster replied. "In river always. Live. Die. Live again. *Never* lie. *Humans* lie! Humans *steal!*"

"And then show up to make the exchange anyway," said Zhang, his voice dripping sarcasm. "Right. That makes all kinds of sense."

"Wait," Jeremy said. "What if–"

"There never was a submarine," Dr. Umbra said, his voice somehow retaining its eerie whispering quality even when he raised it to interrupt. "Greenclaws just wanted to lure us into a trap that would give it even more fresh meat to eat. And we walked right into it, didn't we, monster? Your spawn are all around us."

Greenclaws hesitated. "Spawn here. But–"

Dr. Umbra teleported his pistols into his black-gloved hands and marched right up to the giant creature with both guns extended. "You have until the count of three to call them off," he said. "After that, I'm going to kill you. One, two–"

Greenclaws roared, lunged, and slashed with a huge clawed hand.

*

Matt had come back to the river with a basic–or half-assed–plan: Make sure that when the sub turned up missing, a fight broke out. Then make sure the prisoners escaped in the confusion.

Somehow he'd fumbled his way to accomplishing the first part. He just hadn't expected he'd need to park himself right in front of Greenclaws to do it, or that the monster would swing at him in a horizontal arc rather than downward like it had at Death Metal.

Caught by surprise, he just managed to leap back out of the way. Greenclaws instantly started to snatch for him with the other hand. Then the Bear Killer boomed, and the monster lurched off balance. Matt willed himself invisible and scrambled out of its path.

People shouted and screamed, and AK-47s rattled. Matt spun to check out the overall situation.

Most of the WMDs were attacking Greenclaws. Riflemen blazed away at it. Sweet Lady Q threw a dazzling twist of lightning. With a groan of tortured steel, Death Metal's ability picked up a crane and threw it. Crimson flashes of Freakmaker's power turned patches of the giant creature's scales into open sores or warty lumps. Zhang charged with a sword in either hand.

Which was all fine, but meanwhile, spawn were rushing in. A few of the non-powered gang members, including the pair nearest the prisoners, were shooting at them, but since Matt had previously failed to kill such a monster even when using Dr. Umbra's gun, he doubted assault rifles were going to have an easy time of it, either.

He ran toward the captives, glimpsed a flash of motion from the corner of his eye, and threw himself flat. Tumbling end over end, a Coke machine flew over him. For an instant, he thought Death Metal had intentionally tried to take his head off, then remembered he was still invisible. Naturally, that increased the risk of getting hit by friendly fire.

Still, he stayed that way. To make sure the spawn shambling ever nearer to the prisoners wouldn't see him coming.

As he reached the guards, he said, "Stop shooting," and they both jumped at the sound of Dr. Umbra's sinister whisper. "I've got this." Then he strode on the past them toward the monsters. Though torn and bloody, each of the spawn came on faster now that they didn't have bullets battering and piercing them anymore.

Matt planted himself right in front of the horror in the lead and fired both pistols into its snarling face. Flesh and gore splashed, bone crunched, and the spawn fell over backward with its skull smashed out of shape.

The other creature faltered. Matt stepped forward and blasted twin shots into its face before it could recover from its surprise. It went down, too, and he grinned. Maybe he was actually getting the hang of this.

Making himself visible, he turned and dashed back to the guards. "Head shots," he snapped, pointing to a trio of spawn hauling themselves up out of the water. "Kill those next. Then the ones to the right of them."

The WMDs exchanged glances and then did as instructed.

As he stood and fired alongside them, Matt silently urged the prisoners to start running. *I cleared a path for you,* he thought. *I've got the guards looking in the other direction. Go for it!*

And eventually, they did. Because he was waiting for it, he noticed, but, scared and intent on their monstrous targets, deafened by the thunder of the Bear Killer, the clatter of the assault rifles, the rasp and crash of metal, and the sizzle of lightning bolts, the thugs were oblivious.

Once the captives were away, Matt ran to Freakmaker, who stood with his upraised arms glowing red to the elbows, the light shining through the fabric of his coat. The villain pivoted, revealing the sweat on his face and the rage and frustration in his scowl.

"Forget Greenclaws," said Matt. "Zap the spawn!"

"You don't tell me what to do!"

"Your power isn't really hurting Greenclaws. The thing's too big for you. But you *can* get the spawn, and one of us supers needs to. The riflemen can't hold them back by themselves."

Freakmaker made a disgusted spitting sound. Then he turned, scarlet light flashed from his fingertips, and lengths of bone jabbed out of a spawn's body and twisted around it like vines. Hobbled and bound by its own substance, it tripped and fell on its face.

Good, Matt thought. But unfortunately, it still didn't look like the rest of the WMDs were making much progress with the biggest threat of all.

Svergr had disappeared from the end of the dock. Zhang was slashing at Greenclaws's feet, but even the magic of chi didn't allow him to slice deep enough to cripple them. Ignoring the harassment, flailing and floundering through a barrage of steel struts, lead pipe, and bright, snaking bursts of electricity, the monster lumbered closer and closer to Death Metal and Sweet Lady Q.

It was also lurching along the facade of a warehouse. Matt sprinted between Greenclaws and the WMDs. A blast from his gun threw a door open, and he scrambled on into the building.

The interior was all one open space with a high ceiling. Wrought-iron stairs climbed to some sort of loft. They clanked as he ran upward.

The loft had a couple office cubicles, a break area with a table, chairs, sink, refrigerator, and microwave, but was mostly additional storage space. A row of windows extended along the wall. Matt looked out and saw he was on approximately the same level as Greenclaws's head. Maybe close enough to do some damage.

He wished himself invisible, ran to one of the windows and fired both rayguns at a round black eye, the twin pulses of force smashing the pane on their way to the target. At once, he scurried to a different window. If he kept dodging back and forth, Greenclaws shouldn't be able to get a fix on him.

That plan worked for two more shots. Then, roaring, the monster started smashing the entire upper portion of the building. Chunks of brick flew through the air as enormous hands with webbed fingers clawed right through the wall. The same raking swings jolted the floor and tore sections loose to plummet through the open space below. Barely able to keep his balance, Matt staggered toward the stairs. He wondered if he could reach them before the whole loft fell. At the moment, it wasn't looking good.

*

Death Metal was standing his ground, and, panting with an unaccustomed fear, Antoinette did, too. Partly out of loyalty, partly out of stubbornness, and partly because she figured Greenclaws would kill them in a heartbeat if they were stupid enough to turn their backs.

Where was Svergr? She'd seen when a couple spawn scrambled up onto the dock behind him, grabbed him, and manhandled him into the water, but he was supposed to have a rebreather in his helmet. He needed to deal with the lesser monsters and bring the Bear Killer back to the *real* fight.

Dr. Umbra ran around her. She gasped and, clenching, held in the bolt she'd been on the very verge of throwing. He blew open a door and darted inside.

She found out why when shots started crashing through a row of upper-story windows. Greenclaws faltered in its advance and clapped a hand over its eye. Then it pivoted and smashed at the upper portion of building.

"Good," Clarence said. "Fall back."

"Wait!" Antoinette gasped. "While it's distracted, can you stick some metal to its foot?"

"I can try," Clarence said, turning toward the broken pieces of the crane he'd thrown early on in the battle. They jumped into the air, flew at Greenclaws, and twisted around the bottom of its leg like ankle bracelets. Zhang leaped back so they wouldn't hit him.

Antoinette sprinted forward and grabbed hold of one of the pieces with both hands. She could fling a lot of juice through empty air, but she could pump even more through a good conductor.

And now she drove it in until her insides ached and she cried out. Meanwhile, Greenclaws stood rigid and shuddering. Smoke and the stench of charring flesh filled the air.

When the flow of power gave out, the monster's body toppled like a felled tree, and, exhausted though she was, Antoinette scurried to make sure it didn't land on top of her. After that, she had to flop down on a box.

Luckily, nobody needed her to do anything more strenuous. Peering around, she saw the fight was over. Greenclaws looked pretty well cooked, and if there were any spawn left alive, they'd apparently run away when their master dropped.

A few moments later, Svergr hauled himself back onto the dock. She was glad to see he was all right, and glad again when Dr. Umbra stepped out of the half-demolished warehouse.

"Apparently, we won," the vigilante whispered.

Death Metal gave him an irritated look. "We didn't get a submarine, and our prisoners escaped. A poor excuse for a victory, if you ask me."

Dr. Umbra shrugged. "I guess it's all in how you look at it."

Adaptation

Matt crept toward the bowling alley. The wasps had been fairly quiet lately. Still, that was no guarantee they hadn't raided here in his absence, or that they weren't lurking here now.

His night vision spotted the human sentry gnawing on a Slim Jim inside a minivan. Plainly, there were still survivors holed up in the building.

That meant there was no reason Matt absolutely had to keep sneaking, except that he had a hunch Dr. Umbra had never simply walked in and out of anyplace. He'd appeared suddenly and vanished mysteriously. If Matt wanted to go on impersonating him, he probably needed to do the same.

He swung wide around the minivan, cracked open the front door of the bowling alley, and peeked through. Nobody was looking in his direction—at this time of night, most people were sleeping on benches or the floor—so he eased on inside.

It was almost as dark inside as out, with just a couple lanterns burning to alleviate the gloom. One was on a table in the snack bar, and Bradley, a sour-looking older man with scraggly white old-man eyebrows, was sitting next to it. His lips moved as he poured over his Bible.

Matt crept close enough to catch the sour smell of his BO— the invasion hadn't improved anybody's personal hygiene—and whispered, "Hello."

He felt a little bad about it when Bradley jerked around in his chair, and worse when the guy stared at him with wide-eyed fear. Creepy was one thing, but he didn't want to give anybody a heart attack.

"It's all right," he said. "It's me, Dr. Umbra. A friend."

Bradley swallowed. "Uh...yes. I see."

"If Ms. Hollingsworth awake? I'd like to speak with her."

"She...I know she'd want to talk to you. Come on."

Bradley led him to the door of the office that had once belonged to the owner or manager of the bowling alley. Over time, this particular band of survivors had elected Sally to be its leader, but her own little room was the only special perk she'd claimed for herself.

Bradley knocked. Sally answered with a groggy-sounding "What?"

"Dr. Umbra's here," Bradley said.

Matt heard movement, something that might be a drawer sliding open and shut, and then the nurse answered the door. The blond tint was coming out of her tousled brown hair. She'd been sleeping in her clothes like everyone did anymore, but her feet were bare. A few flecks of red polish still clung to the nails.

"It's been a while," she said, her voice and expression somber. "We were starting to worry."

"I meant to come back sooner, but other things got in the way. What do you need? How can I help you?"

"Come in, and we'll talk about it." She kicked a sleeping bag and air mattress up against the wall and waved him to a chair beside the desk. The light spilling through the door gleamed on framed team photos and individual shots of guys displaying the rings they'd earned for bowling perfect games.

As Matt sat down, Sally said, "Let me light a candle." She circled around behind him toward a shelf where a couple of them sat, the bottom of each glued to a saucer with wax. Then something round and hard jabbed the back of his neck, and, startled, he jumped the same way Bradley had.

"It's a gun," Sally said. "If you move, turn invisible, or do anything, I'll pull the trigger."

"This is why Bradley was so nervous," he said, feeling stupid, "even after he knew it was me. And why you didn't act glad to see me."

"Can you blame us?" she replied.

"Yes! Because I don't understand."

She reached over his head and dropped a piece of paper on the desk in front of him. "Pick it up slowly," she said.

The flyer was hand-written in marker. The heading read *News and Warnings,* and most of the text beneath reported that Dr. Umbra had joined the WMDs, and then the gang had rounded up people to give to the man-eating monster Greenclaws to seal a bargain. Fortunately, the deal had fallen apart, but the story made it clear that in no way absolved the supervillains of guilt for what they'd intended.

Damn it! Matt thought. Why hadn't he seen this coming? But then again, why would he? It wasn't like he ever anticipated anything else.

He set the flyer back down. "I can explain."

"Then do it," Sally said. "Explain joining a gang of criminals and capturing people to be slaughtered."

"When the wasps attacked, all the heroes—all but me, I mean—went down fighting. The villains didn't. They didn't care about protecting innocent people, so they hid. Now they're the only ones left with superpowers, and our only hope of beating the invaders is to use them."

"So you made peace with them."

"Only to a point. I was never going to let Greenclaws eat those people. I'm the one who sabotaged the deal and made sure the prisoners escaped. Gwen Porter—the girl who writes the flyers—just didn't realize it because I had to be sneaky."

Sally hesitated. Then: "What about everything else the WMDs do? According to what we've heard, they treat the people in their territory like slaves."

Matt sighed. "I know. But I can't fix every problem at the same time."

"What if I let you leave here and you tell Death Metal and his friends that they should bring *us* under their control?"

"If I want that, why haven't I done it already? Look, I may be some mysterious phantom to everybody else, but you know me now, don't you, at least a little? We got these people out of the hive together. We've taken care of them since. Do you *really* believe I've gone bad?"

For a moment, the room was quiet. Then a match scratched on a striking pad, its acrid smell tinged the air, and Sally really did light a candle. She closed the door, went behind the desk, sat, and laid down her stainless steel S&W Model 669.

"Sorry," she said.

"It's okay. I get it. The important thing is, now you know we're still on the same side."

"Yes, but no one else does. Which I guess is a good thing."

"Wait. What?"

She smiled a smile that looked as tired as he felt. "If you're sure this–pretending to throw in with the criminals–is the right move, then you can't do it halfway. You can't be the guardian angel of the survivors in one part of town and a villain someplace else. The WMDs will hear about it, and then where will you be?"

He hesitated. "If I'm careful, I can at least go on helping our group."

"No, you can't. We trade information and supplies with other survivors. There's too much risk that somebody, one of the children, maybe, would let the secret slip."

An aching, empty feeling welled up inside him. After a moment, he identified it as loneliness, or the fear of it. It didn't matter that since finding the costume, he'd tried to act as cold and aloof as the real Dr. Umbra. He'd still fought for and alongside Sally and her people. He'd shared their water, food, and various places of refuge, their fear, grief, and fleeting moments of happiness. They'd become his second family whether they realized it or not.

Now all he'd have was his camaraderie with Sweet Lady Q and Zhang Sanfeng, and that was a friendship tainted by deeper lies than simply stealing a dead hero's identity.

Still, Sally was right, so there was nothing to do but suck it up. He looked at her and said, "I'll still look out for everyone. You just won't see me doing it. And when I find out something you need to know, like where there's food or what the wasps are doing, I'll sneak in and tell you without anybody else realizing I'm around."

"Thank you."

"So, how did I get out of here tonight? I guess you got the drop on me and made me confess to joining the WMDs, but then, somehow, I turned invisible and slipped away before you could shoot me."

Sally smiled. "That sounds like the kind of thing you'd do."

*

Matt hated the way the store looked. His apartment had usually been a mess, but he'd urged his team to keep this place neat and clean. Partly to attract customers, rack up strong sales figures, and eventually move up to district manager, but also because, for whatever reason, it had felt worth doing for its own sake.

Now, parts of the roof had fallen, rain had poured in through the holes, and of course the store had been looted. He'd done it himself, bringing Sally and her people here to carry away guns, ammunition, bows and arrows, camping gear, baseball bats to use as clubs, football helmets and pads to serve as body armor, and anything else that might conceivably help them survive.

So at this point, whether people were looking for shelter or supplies, there was little reason for them to come in here or stick around if they did, and that, Matt had figured, made it a good place to hide something. He strode to a display of golf bags, pulled out one in the back, upended it, and dumped out Red Bear's claw-studded leather wristbands.

As soon as he picked them up, he felt the same dizzying rush of emotion as before. He perceived himself to be in the presence of something vast and wonderful, like the ocean. But there was also a sense of hovering on the very brink of danger, like holding his hand just outside a lion's cage. If he stretched it out just a tiny bit further and let it slip between the bars at all, the beast would grab it and rip it off.

"Damn it," he muttered, "what am I supposed to do?"

"I am available for consultation," a voice replied.

Startled, Matt whirled, looking for the source, and then belatedly recognized the calm, intellectual tones. Slumping, he said, "Solomon. You're back."

"I am."

"Are you fixed?"

"Possibly. I now infer that in addition to damaging my hardware, the aliens infected me with a virus, although it is unclear how they could have accomplished such a thing. Diagnostics indicate I have deleted the hostile influence, but only time will tell for certain."

Matt sighed. "So you're saying, talk fast."

"That may prove advantageous. You are contemplating Red Bear's regalia."

"If that's what you call them. What would happen if I put them on?"

"Conjecture: You would either die, go insane, or acquire Red Bear's abilities."

Matt snorted. "Thanks. That really narrows it down. What would determine which of those things happened?"

"Conjecture: Either a supernatural entity's attitude toward you or your innate spiritual resilience."

"What do you know that *isn't* 'conjecture?'"

"Relatively little. My database encompasses Qabala, Wicca, Voodoo, and Satanism among other esoteric doctrines and disciplines, but Red Bear's abilities did not appear to derive from any of them, nor was he ever forthcoming about the actual source. Because we do not understand the wristbands, I recommend handling them with circumspection."

"So you wouldn't just yank them on and hope for the best."

"I would not."

"Okay, but here's the thing. Dr. Umbra's abilities are amazing. But you said yourself that the wasps may be breeding a special kind of hunter to take away his edge."

"I did?"

Matt sighed. "Trust me, yeah, you did. And even if they aren't, I don't have enough power to go head to head with a whole army of aliens."

"Over the course of his career, Dr. Umbra defeated many formidable adversaries."

"Because he knew what he was doing. I don't. But Red Bear didn't need a lot of skills and tricks. He could just punch through whatever got in his way."

"You will recall that ultimately, the invaders killed him."

Matt hesitated. "Yeah. Okay. There's that. But I still need more power than I've got."

"Recommendation: You should come to the Castle."

"The what?"

"My physical location. The secret headquarters of the superheroes of Jackson City. As I endeavored to repair myself, I also worked to make the base accessible once more."

Matt grinned. "That's great! I'd like to see it. But what's it got to do with what we're talking about?"

"Three things: A human operator may be able to assist me if the virus returns. I can attempt to repair the phasing function of your cloak and acquaint you with the full range of the Castle's resources, at which point you may decide you do not require Red Bear's abilities after all. And should you still insist on donning the wristbands, he created a sort of shrine here. It may be the optimal place to do so."

"Sounds good." Matt shoved the wristbands into his pockets. "Give me directions."

*

The first thing it perceived was the cold.

Cold which was less intense than it had been. Otherwise, it couldn't have perceived anything. But the cold still held it, in weakness, sluggishness, and the threat of dormancy.

So the prisoner reached inside itself and slowly reconfigured certain mechanisms. Initially intended for mobility and attack, they now became furnaces.

But they failed to burn hot enough. The cold crippled them as it paralyzed the entity of which they were a part.

Recognizing that they were overmatched, the prisoner resumed its computations. Even thought crept and faltered, hindered by the cold, but eventually, it arrived at an augmented strategy.

It reached deeper into itself, and, like cancer, micro-nanites roused. The tiny machines rebuilt nuclei to create isotopes with extremely short half-lives. As those artificial elements decayed, they warmed the furnaces, and when the furnaces burned hotter, they thawed the prisoner.

That brought other functions online. The prisoner perceived its captivity more clearly. It recognized the program laboring to monitor and chill it.

That program was already faltering due to some difficulty the prisoner couldn't yet perceive. It was vulnerable, and although energy was still in short supply, formulating and transmitting a chain of poison code hardly required any at all.

Once the laser-cooling process halted, it was only a matter of time before the prisoner's batteries generated sufficient energy to shape the appurtenances needed to attack the titanium-alloy and plastic container. With pincers, a pry bar, and a cutting torch, it worked until a window fell clattering from its frame.

Then it hopped to the floor and assessed.

It was in a large room filled with a miscellany of objects and containers. Although grinding and thumping noises echoed in from elsewhere, there were no living organisms or active machines in view, and thus, no immediate danger.

The absence of threat afforded the escapee the opportunity to take stock of its internal state. It had fulfilled the Escape imperative, and thus it would now have addressed a Mission imperative except that none such existed in memory. By default, then, it would go to Roving Standby mode.

It evacuated the remaining isotopes whose radioactivity might otherwise have ultimately impaired its functioning. That took less time than transmuting them back into something innocuous. It repurposed the pincers and pry bar into forelegs and the cutting torch into a weapon. That returned it to its basic form, a quadripedal box with a swivel-mounted heat ray on its back. Then it started wandering and surveying its surroundings in more detail.

It spotted the source of the noise as soon as it exited the hall in which it had awakened. Something had damaged this complex, and robots, some humanoid, others not, labored to effect repairs.

They didn't take any notice of the escapee, but that could conceivably change. It scanned them and found that, although capable of a measure of autonomy, they, like the program that had governed the refrigerated cage, were ultimately extensions of the ruling intelligence of this place. That meant they shared its current susceptibility to tampering, and the escapee ensured its continued unobtrusiveness with another squirt of toxic code.

Then, patient, tireless, but most of all ready, it wandered.

*

Matt stared at the stars and swirls of incandescent gas blazing in the air before him. There was no doubt he was in superhero land now. First, a secret door in the basement of a graffiti-covered tenement had led him to a plastic cylinder with a seat inside it. Then the cylinder took him on a hurtling, plunging ride through a looping underground tube that reminded him of making a deposit at the drive-through window of a bank. Now there was this, just a few steps away from the little platform where the vigilantes' private subway car had dropped him off.

"Nice," he said. "What is that, a hologram of the galaxy?"

"Of a portion of our spiral arm of it," Solomon replied. "The planetarium *can* display the entire galaxy, or every known galaxy, but since most of the extraterrestrials known to humanity came from star systems close to our own, the heroes deemed this to be the most generally useful scale."

"Well, whatever it is, it's an impressive thing to see as soon as you walk in the front door."

"You did not come in via the primary entrance," the AI said, "nor is ostentation the reason the planetarium occupies this particular space. The Castle has several points of ingress, and grew somewhat haphazardly as its creators chose to add one sort of area or another. Everything is quite functional, or was before the bombardment, but you may discern a certain randomness to the overall layout."

"I understand. You want to give me the grand tour?"

"As you wish. Proceed through the doorway in the far wall."

Matt headed straight across the room. It was fun to step right through shining clouds and have stars burning on every side.

Beyond the planetarium were clear walls with strange plants growing behind them. In one enclosure, the ragged leaves were mostly orange. In another, orchids blew iridescent bubbles. In a third, illuminated by a blue glow, spindly trees fumbled at their neighbors like lethargic monkeys grooming one another.

"These are from outer space," Matt said, and then, inwardly wincing, silently added, *duh*.

"Yes," Solomon answered. "Fortunately, the bombardment did not breach the habitats. Otherwise, emergency sterilization would have occurred to keep the contents from contaminating the terrestrial biosphere."

As the tour continued, Solomon showed him chemical and forensic laboratories, a miniature hospital, machine shops, a weight room with barbells and machines for people with superhuman strength, and a dojo with mats on the floor and racks of staves, shinai, and real swords on the walls. There was even a cavernous vault containing a whole fake city block where animatronics, some making simulated attacks and others representing hostages and other innocent civilians, popped out unexpectedly, and a hero could practice climbing, swinging on a line, or maneuvering in flight without smacking into a wall.

As the AI had warned, the complex was a maze, and Matt soon lost his bearings even though he was only seeing a portion of it. He wondered how much more was currently inaccessible, and how long it would take Solomon's machines to get those sections opened up again.

One of those machines was currently working inside an elevator shaft. The clatter and whir of its tools sounded through the open door. Another gadget the size of a cat stood just outside in the adjacent corridor, contributing nothing to the repair effort as far as Matt could tell.

A moment after he noticed it, the thing turned. Since it had no head, it took Matt a moment to be sure it actually had turned *toward* him. Then he spotted the two round lenses in the near end of it. It was looking at him just like he was looking at it.

But why? It made him uneasy even though he figured there was really no reason to be. "Solomon?" he said.

"I am here," the computer answered. "Shall I repeat or elaborate on the last set of directions?"

"No. It isn't that. Why is your little friend staring–"

The rod on the machine's back swiveled.

Matt turned invisible, jumped a pistol into his hand, and dodged, all at once. A split second later, he realized he'd been paranoid. But he'd learned to react as he had whenever a wasp pointed a raygun at him, and the metal appendage on the robot's back bore a resemblance to a weapon.

A *strong* resemblance, actually. The end glowed red, and a thin beam stabbed through the space Matt had just vacated. It instantly charred a spot on the wall, and then he fired back.

The blast from Dr. Umbra's pistol crumpled the little machine and hurled it rolling and clanging across the floor. It tumbled into the open elevator shaft and plummeted out of sight.

Okay, Matt thought, reappearing. *that was easy, but also weird.* "What the hell?" he asked.

"Please explain why you activated your invisibility and discharged your weapon," Solomon replied.

"Because your gadget shot at me first!"

"I do not understand. You did not appear to be firing at anything in particular."

Matt used his pistol to point at the burn mark on the wall. "Is that 'anything in particular?'"

"Assessing," Solomon said, and then, after a pause, "Please describe the mechanism in question."

"It looked like an aluminum mailbox with legs and a heat ray on top."

Something banged inside the elevator shaft and made him jump. Then the car plunged through the open space with a robot smashed to the underside of it. An even louder crash sounded from the bottom a second later.

"What's happening?" Matt asked. "Are all your machines going crazy?"

"No," Solomon said. "The robot that shot at you was not one of mine, and I dropped the elevator on it deliberately in hopes of slowing it down."

Matt cocked his head. "That seems like overkill. It wasn't very tough. If my shot didn't wreck it, the fall probably finished it off."

"That is unlikely," the computer said. "It was designed to weather seemingly catastrophic damage. After each such setback, it analyzes what has just befallen it and uses the data to reconstruct itself with augmentation."

"You sound like you know what it is."

"It is Tabula Rasa. The late roboticist Calvin Otto created the various iterations of the device to serve as his assassins."

"If he's 'the late,' what's it doing here?"

"Conjecture: This is the Tabula Rasa previously displayed in the trophy room. To facilitate its escape from confinement, it infected me with the virus I erroneously attributed to the extraterrestrials. This accounts for my failure to register its absence or directly perceive it even now."

"What does it want?"

"Conjecture: Prior to encountering you, it had no objective beyond preserving its freedom of movement, but Calvin Otto programmed it to stalk and kill Dr. Umbra on sight."

"Of course he did. How do we destroy it for real?"

"That is uncertain. Its cage kept it inactive in its original form by maintaining it at a temperature of one hundred picokelvins. It is possible..."

"What is?" Matt asked. "What's a picokelvin? Tell me!"

Solomon didn't answer. Matt could only assume the virus had crippled the AI yet again.

That decided him on what to do next: catch the next cylinder out of here. He was probably going to have to destroy Tabula Rasa eventually, but the smart play was to put it off until Solomon resumed talking and could coach him through it.

What was the shortest way to an exit? He was still trying to choose a direction when Tabula Rasa heaved itself back up into the elevator doorway.

Solomon had warned that the killer robot would rebuild itself every time someone crippled it. The AI hadn't mentioned that the machine would latch onto whatever parts were handy to do it, but that was evidently the case. Tabula Rasa was bigger now, with a manlike shape, and, for the most part, a blue finish like the mechanical repairman the plunging elevator had swept down the shaft.

Matt turned invisible, sidestepped, and fired. With a clank, the blast pounded a dent in Tabula Rasa's torso but failed to smash it or throw it down the shaft like before. The robot had stronger armor now and had hold of the frame around the door, too, its fingertips digging in.

Its eyes flared red, and its head pivoted back and forth, rapidly and unpredictably, flashing rays in a wide arc. Matt dived beneath the barrage, jumped his other pistol into his off hand, and fired both at the robot's neck.

That bashed its head back and angled its eyes toward the ceiling. It stuck that way, too, but its insides were already humming as it sought to repair and perhaps improve itself.

Matt fired twin blasts at one steel hand and then the other. The pistols smashed off some fingers and twisted and flattened the rest. Then he tried another body shot, and, unable to maintain its hold, the machine fell backward and out of sight once more.

The second exchange still hadn't been as tough as some other fights Matt had survived. It had been harder than the first one, though, and if he allowed Tabula Rasa to catch up with him again, the next one was bound to be rougher still. He reappeared and ran.

A wrong turn brought him to the dead end of a collapsed tunnel. He spun around and tried another path. It led him through a spacious area furnished with a wet bar, ping-pong, billiard, and foosball tables, pinball machines, arcade games, and a big flat-screen TV. He supposed this was where the superheroes had come for R&R, and he wondered fleetingly if even the creepy Dr. Umbra had occasionally unwound with a beer or a little Xbox.

Then, beyond a doorway, he spotted another little platform with a cylinder waiting to take him somewhere. He didn't care where. Even if it dumped him off right under the floating hive-ship, that would be safer than staying here.

Fortunately, there was nothing to operating the cars. You got in, sat down, fastened your seat belt, and pushed the big green button. Then the gull-wing door closed, and the cylinder whisked you off to wherever.

Except, not this time.

He mashed the button repeatedly, but the car wouldn't move. Apparently, by interfering with Solomon's brain, Tabula Rasa had taken the system offline.

The robot appeared at the far end of the heroes' rec room. It had sucked up more metal from somewhere and made itself bulkier.

Matt wondered if it had upgraded its senses, too. Would his invisibility still work against it?

There was one way to find out. Unwilling to stay penned in the cylinder while Tabula Rasa prowled closer, he made himself vanish and slipped back onto the platform.

The mechanical assassin pivoted in his direction. Its eyes glowed red.

Matt dropped, and the fan-shaped barrage of heat rays burned over him. Instantly, Tabula Rasa's neck telescoped a couple inches and bent like a gooseneck lamp, angling its head for a burst that would pepper the surface of the platform.

The cylinder nearly filled the tunnel in which it ran, but there was a narrow space between its curved, clear surface and the wall. Matt scrambled, jammed himself into it, and stuck. Snarling, he squirmed and strained and popped on through.

Afterward, panting, he felt clever, or might have if it had been calculation instead of pure frightened desperation that had prompted him to act as he had. By rebuilding itself in such a massive form, Tabula Rasa had grown too big to follow him. Now he'd simply hike to the end of the tunnel on foot and escape back into the city above. He killed his invisibility and started to jog.

There was another little platform up ahead, another way in and out of the Castle. It seemed impossible that the robot could have already raced the long way round to wait in ambush there, but he resolved to approach cautiously nonetheless.

Then something hummed. A slight vibration quivered through the tube, and he belatedly realized that if Tabula Rasa could turn off the cylinder system, maybe it could switch it back on as well.

He sprinted. At his back, the car hurtled up the tunnel with a *swoosh* like a swinging blade.

He reached the platform and heaved himself onto the top of it. *Instantly,* the car shot past the platform. Displaced air, or maybe his own headlong momentum and lack of balance, knocked him staggering and lashed Dr. Umbra's cloak around him.

God, that was close! Still, he couldn't stand here and wait for his heart to stop hammering. Since he couldn't escape out the tubes, he had to keep moving through the Castle, staying ahead of Tabula until he found a way to shut it down for good.

He scurried down another corridor. "Solomon," he whispered, "can you hear me?"

"Yes, Doctor," the computer replied.

"I'm *not*...skip it. Tabula Rasa is chasing me. Can you see it?"

"No. Assessing."

"Don't bother. Take my word for it, you've got a virus. Check and see if you can take back control of the cylinder cars."

"Assessing: Not at this time. It is curious that, although unoccupied, they are all in motion."

"To run me over if I go into the tubes. Look, you said that before, you kept Tabula locked up at a certain temperature?"

"Yes. Magnetar demonstrated mathematically that even a cybernetic system as adaptable as Tabula Rasa could not function at a temperature verging on absolute zero. Thus, it was practical to preserve one iteration of the device for study and display."

"Right. It's working out great so far."

A metallic figure stepped out of a doorway ahead. Startled, Matt nearly started blasting before he saw it was just another repair robot.

He took a deep breath. "So," he continued, "if we cool Tabula way, way down, that'll shut it off?"

"Perhaps, but it is uncertain how quickly I can recover control of the cooling-laser array. Even assuming I can do so expeditiously, you, Doctor, would need to replace Tabula Rasa in its container and hold it there while the lasers performed their function. Has it enlarged itself since it began stalking you?"

"Yeah. It's bigger than me now.

"Then it is also larger than the space it formerly occupied."

"Damn it! What else have you got that's really cold? How about liquid oxygen? It worked on the Terminator."

"It is doubtful the quantity available could achieve the desired effect. Note, too, that it is not present in a weaponized form."

Matt peeked around a corner. Striding with a silence that seemed like cheating in something so big, metallic, and heavy, Tabula Rasa was just a few yards down the corridor that ran at right angles to his own.

Matt's first impulse was to flee back the way he'd come, but there was nothing in that direction that could help him. Praying it would protect him at least a little, he turned invisible and crept into the intersection.

Tabula Rasa's eyes flared red. Matt lunged forward and out of the robot's line of sight just in time to avoid the pulses of searing heat.

He had to take cover! He looked around and realized his prowling had brought him back to the chamber containing the fake city block. Reappearing, he dashed through the entrance, and all the funhouse machinery came to life. Recorded gunfire, screams, and sirens sounded through the streets. The smell of gun smoke tinged the air.

Ignoring the animatronic figures that popped up and shot blanks, dodging around the ones that lurched into his path, he ducked into a bar and kept moving toward the back. The mechanical thugs seated in a booth reached into their jackets.

"Solomon!" he whispered. "Are you in control of the repair robots?"

"I presently control the majority."

"How are they at knocking down something really big and solid? Can they do it fast?"

"If they use explosives, and if it is unnecessary to collapse the object in question with precision, they conceivably can."

"Then here's the plan. There's a big art deco-looking building in the center of the block."

"The Hawthorne Building."

"Whatever. I'm going to lure Tabula to the top of it. Then, when I tell you, you bring the whole thing down. If you can knock down the ones to either side and dump them on top of it, so much the better."

"That is unlikely to destroy Tabula Rasa."

"I get that, but if we bury it alive—or whatever—won't that at least slow it down?"

"Possibly. The robots are acquiring explosives from the stores. They will proceed as you direct."

Matt found a back way out of the bar, cut through an alley, and skulked up the space between two buildings. Even here, sudden noise jolted him, and animatronics jumped out of nowhere to test his reactions. He hoped it was all as much of a distraction for his pursuer as it was for him.

Maybe it was. When he peeked back out at the street, Tabula Rasa was crouching just inside the exit to the corridor, where it had apparently decided an upgrade was in order. Buzzing and humming, the robot had gathered several of the bad-guy animatronics and connected itself to them with thick cables. The animatronics dwindled like melting candles or deflating balloons while Tabula grew larger and dropped to all fours. New heads humped up from its back to glare red-eyed in all directions, and new limbs sprouted from its flanks. Most of the latter terminated in hands gripping pistols, shotguns, and rifles.

Matt skulked back the way he'd come, circled around, and found a back way into the Hawthorne Building. Willing himself invisible, he crept to the front of the lobby, pointed his pistols at Tabula Rasa, and fired. The twin pulses smashed one of the windows in front of him.

Then he whirled and dived behind a reception desk, and not an instant too soon. More plate glass shattered, and bits of wall charred, as Tabula returned fire.

Matt peeked over the top of the desk. Its upgrade evidently complete, or at least complete enough, Tabula came scuttling up the street like a bug.

Keeping low, Matt scurried to the door that led to the service stairs. "Solomon!" he said. "Tabula's following me into ground zero. Move your workers!"

He waited until Tabula crawled through the shattered windows, snapped off a shot to get its attention, then whirled and ran up the steps. The robot's return fire cracked and clattered against the door swinging shut behind him.

Tabula's bulk hindered it as it climbed. Matt could hear it scraping and crunching against the particleboard on the walls of the stairwell. But despite the tight quarters, it sounded like it wasn't more than a flight behind him.

He burst out onto the flat gravel roof of the building, ran to the edge, and balked. Presumably, Dr. Umbra had practiced leaping from roof to roof in this very spot. That didn't mean Matt could do it, and if he screwed up, Tabula wouldn't need to kill him. The five-story fall would do the job.

Still, the sound of the robot forcing its way steadily higher told him he had no choice. He backed up, sprinted, sprang onto the low parapet, and leaped.

The moment he spent in the air seemed to last a long time. Then he jolted down on the roof of the Hawthorne Building's neighbor and pitched forward onto his knees.

He looked around just as Tabula Rasa burst out into the open. Crimson eyes glowing, the robot's various heads turned in his direction. So did its various guns.

"Blow the building!" Matt gasped.

Something boomed. The structure underneath Matt shuddered. Then, with a drawn-out crashing roar, the Hawthorne Building collapsed, carrying Tabula Rasa down into billowing dust and tumbling rubble.

"Yes!" Matt snarled.

"It would be hazardous to demolish the adjacent structures while you are atop one of them," Solomon said.

"What? Oh, right." As he turned off his invisibility, Matt considered making his departure like a sane person. But he wanted all this weight to crash down on top of Tabula right now, and he'd made the jump once, hadn't he?

He stood up, took a deep breath, ran, and long-jumped as he had before. This time, the next roof over was several feet lower, and he slammed down on top of it that much harder, but still without breaking or spraining anything.

"I'm clear," he gasped, turning.

With more thunderous booms and grinding crashes, the Hawthorne Building's neighbors collapsed. Solomon's workers had evidently placed the charges differently, and these two structures didn't drop straight down like the first one had. Instead, breaking apart as they fell, they toppled sideways like trees to bury the wreckage of the original demolition in additional debris.

"Beautiful," Matt said.

"Thank you," the AI replied. "Please do bear in mind that this is not a permanent solution."

Matt looked around and found the stairs that led down into the building. "Maybe not, but I'll take it. Tabula isn't on my tail anymore, and you and I have time to think of something that *will* be permanent."

There was a bank of elevators on the top floor, and Matt decided he'd be happy to ride one down. Tabula had already given him his workout for the day.

"Here's what I'm thinking," he said as the door slid shut and he pressed the "G" button. "If we can't refreeze Tabula or just beat the hell out of it, maybe you can screw with its programming the same way it screwed with yours. Communication is a two-way street, right?"

One of his former girlfriends had loved saying that. It seemed like it kind of applied.

"That is theoretically possible," Solomon replied, "but we must anticipate sophisticated defenses. From start to finish–"

"But you've *already* started trying to figure out Tabula. You started just a few hours after the invasion." Matt stepped off the elevator.

"I do not understand."

"You've shaken off the virus before. You just don't remember. What's more, you've gotten better at it. The first time, it took you weeks to start talking again. Tonight, it was only a few minutes. There has to be a part of you that already understands a lot."

He stepped outside. A mound of spill from the demolished buildings blocked the way to the door through which he'd entered. No doubt at Solomon's command, a secondary exit swung open at the far end of the fake street.

"That may conceivably be so," Solomon said. "Since the bombardment, my functions have been fragmented. It is a by-product of the same dispersal and redundancy that enabled me to survive at all."

"Can you un-fragment them?"

"To some degree, perhaps, and if a portion of me *has* made significant progress analyzing Tabu–I recommend you flee."

"What?"

"Although I am still unable to perceive Tabula Rasa directly, I detect vibration in the pile of debris. The robot is rebuilding itself, digging its way to freedom, or both."

"Jesus! Already?"

"My projections suggest it will emerge from the pile in less than sixty seconds."

Matt ran. "The heroes kept Tabula," he gritted, "so they must have kept other villains' weapons and gadgets, too."

"Yes," Solomon said. "Such items are in the trophy room, but it is doubtful that any of them can stop Tabula Rasa."

"Well, neither can my pistols! I need to try something! Tell me which way to go, but keep working on Tabula's programming, too!"

He pounded onward. A noise like a drum roll swelled as his back. He realized it was the clatter of Tabula's feet as the robot raced in pursuit.

"I am defining Tabula Rasa's firewall," Solomon said after a while, and then, a few moments later, "I am catching glimpses of Tabula Rasa on my cameras."

"Does that mean you're close to shutting it down?"

"It would be imprudent to assume so."

Matt staggered into the trophy room. It wasn't as big as the vault containing the fake city block, but it was spacious enough to house a Viking longship and a Raggedy Ann the size of Greenclaws, among other exhibits. All the display cases clicked open at once with a hiss of escaping air.

Matt looked around and, amid the dozens of bizarre machines and mannequins in masks and body armor, spotted something that looked familiar. Unless he was mistaken, it was an early model of Svergr's Bear Killer, likely confiscated when a superhero captured him.

He snatched the bazooka-like weapon and flipped the arming switch. The gun whined as it powered up. He pivoted toward the door, and Tabula Rasa charged into view.

Once again, though it had banged-up, crumpled spots and even actual holes in it, the robot was bigger than before, and now looked a little like a cross between a horse and a turtle. Red-eyed heads and jointed arms terminating in either rayguns or firearms that bristled from every inch of the shell.

Matt turned invisible and dodged. Tabula started to compensate. Matt jerked the Bear Killer's trigger.

A dazzling flash of energy crashed into Tabula, jolted it backward, and tore many of its heads and arms away. The robot slumped, and for one wonderful moment, Matt believed Svergr's invention might actually have destroyed it.

Then, despite the new smoking, ragged holes in its chassis and the dangling, clattering scraps, Tabula limped forward, pausing to step on a piece of itself and suck it back into its body through its leg.

Matt hefted the Bear Killer for another shot. Then it hit him: Tabula had *paused*.

He threw the weapon, and it clanged down in front of the robot. Tabula considered it, then extruded a prehensile cable that clamped onto the Bear Killer like a lamprey. The gun started to melt.

Matt tore open another display case, pulled out a helmet with stubby horns and a scalloped crest, and rolled that at Tabula's spindly legs.

"What are you doing?" Solomon asked.

"It's in repair mode, and how can it pass up the chance to suck in all these evil-genius gadgets? I'm buying you time to mess with its brain!"

As it turned out, the trick was good for about twenty seconds, time enough for Matt to throw a collection of glowing rings and an unidentifiable black metal cube after the Bear Killer and the helmet. Then, suddenly, the robot stopped paying any attention to the junk. Its scarlet eyes flared, and its remaining limbs pointed their guns at him in a cascade of motion that reminded him crazily of fans in a stadium doing the wave.

He jumped Dr. Umbra's pistols into his hands. Then Solomon snapped, "Do not shoot!"

Matt just managed to keep from squeezing the triggers. Afterward, he saw that Tabula Rasa had stopped moving.

"You did it!" he said.

"Not yet," Solomon said, and although he had to be imagining it, Matt could have sworn he heard intense concentration or perhaps even strain in that calm, professorial voice. "Please divest yourself of your hat, cloak, mask, gloves, and pistols."

You're kidding, Matt thought. *Throw away every trick I've got?* Yet he did it as quickly as he could, and, leaving the gear in a pile on the floor, backed away.

"Thank you," Solomon said, his voice now coming from a speaker in the nearest wall. "That was helpful. I believe it has enabled me to solve the immediate problem."

Tabula stood and stared at the vigilante's effects for a time. Then bits of metal dropped rustling and clinking away from it like it was shedding skin after skin.

"I could not remove the primary directive to kill Dr. Umbra," Solomon said, "but I could edit Tabula Rasa's memory and impair its ability to identify you. Since it is no longer cognizant of any designated target, it is returning to its standby mode."

Sure enough, when it finished shrinking and simplifying itself, Tabula was a mailbox with legs again. It gave Matt another look, turned, and started to walk away.

"You aren't just going to let it wander around, are you?" he asked.

"No. Now that time no longer presses, I will take the proper measures to return it to dormancy and an appropriate container. I must also inquire who you are and how you came to possess Dr. Umbra's equipment."

Matt sighed. "How did I know you were going to say that?"

*

"I have finished," Solomon said.

Matt pulled the cloak off the table and out from under the various hanging robotic tools. The garment didn't look any different, or feel different when he pulled it on.

"You need only will the phase shift," Solomon said, "in the same way you make yourself invisible."

Okay, Matt thought, *I want to be a ghost.* He stretched out his hand to one of the hanging devices, a laser Solomon had used to open the fabric of the caped coat, perform surgery on the circuitry inside, and seal it up again afterward.

His fingers passed through the spindly, tapered length of metal and plastic without resistance. Hesitantly, fighting his own instinctive conviction that a person couldn't simply walk through solid objects, he eased forward. None of the other hanging instruments impeded him, either, nor did the worktable itself.

"Damn," he breathed.

"There are limitations," Solomon said. "Phasing requires even more energy than invisibility, and while desolid, you cannot affect the material world. Still, the first Dr. Umbra found it a useful capability."

Matt willed himself solid and touched the table to make sure he really was. "I'll bet. It's incredible." He took a breath and squared his shoulders. "But I still need you to show me Red Bear's shrine."

"Please consider that I have already enhanced your powers."

"And don't think I'm not grateful. But you said it yourself. Phasing is like invisibility. It's defense. I need more offense."

"Even without desolidification, your current abilities sufficed to defeat Tabula Rasa."

"*We* defeated Tabula, you more than me, and we were lucky. Anyway, there's more to it than just power. I promised Sally I'd look after her group, but there's only so much I can do without ever letting anybody know I'm around. With Red Bear's wristbands *and* Dr. Umbra's stuff, I can be a real superhero to regular people and a different one, the sellout, when I need to be him."

The shrine turned out to be a square little room, unfurnished except for a hollow log in the center of the floor and drawings in swirls of reddish pigment on the walls. The latter were pretty good in a sketchy cartoon way. Matt spotted deer, a snake, birds, and, as he might have expected, several bears.

"Red Bear used the log as a drum," Solomon said.

Matt nodded. "Should I start out that way?"

"I do not know."

'I'll skip it, then."

He took off Dr. Umbra's costume. He didn't know if he needed to do that, either, but for some reason, it felt right. Then he picked up the first wristband and shivered at the mixture of wonder and dread that pierced him. You'd think he'd get used to it, but he hadn't, not even a little.

Should he do this? He had no idea, but damn it, he was going to. For all the reasons he'd given Solomon, and a couple he hadn't.

Maybe a steely character like Dr. Umbra could have handled being a WMD twenty-four seven. Matt, however, needed the companionship of normal people to keep his head on straight just like desperate survivors needed the hope a superhero could provide. With luck, by impersonating Red Bear, he could help out everybody.

He jerked the wristband on.

Author's Note

What will the wristbands do to Matt?

What will happen when the WMDs turn on him?

What is the wasps' next horrific move?

Is there any hope for Jackson City, or Earth itself, for that matter?

For the answers to these and other questions, tune in next time, same Matt time, same Matt channel!

But seriously...

The Impostor is a superhero comic in prose, a modern hero pulp, and my chance to write a kind of story I've loved all my life. I hope you're having as much fun with it as I am. If so, Matt's adventures continue in *The Impostor: Blood Machine*.

Meanwhile, let me leave you with a bonus story. This one is set in the Impostor universe before the alien invasion and relates an incident from the life of Sweet Lady Q.

The Little Things

Antoinette's chest still ached, and she had a foul, hot chemical taste in her mouth, but she stopped coughing first. Maybe it was because Dr. Umbra had inhaled a bigger dose of toxic smoke carrying her clear of the burning base. Anyway, he was still hacking. He'd even pulled up his black mask to uncover his mouth and nostrils.

Best to slip away before he recovered. She took a step backward and thought she was being quiet. But he lurched around in a swirl of cloak and pointed a raygun. His hand in its dark glove shook.

She called up her power. Electricity shivered inside her like a caffeine buzz, and sparks fell from her fingertips.

I can fry him, she thought. *He's weak*. But she didn't want to anymore. He was a superhero, but he'd risked his life to save hers after her supposed friends and allies abandoned her to die.

Another fit of coughing doubled him over.

"Don't make me hurt you," she said. "I just want out. Let me walk away and I promise nobody will ever hear from Sweet Lady Q again."

He stared at her through one-way lenses. Then the pistol vanished, teleported back to wherever he kept it.

*

The black dye job and the glasses were a disguise, but Cathy still recognized her little sister standing in the yellow glow of the porch light. Her blue eyes widened, and she gasped.

"It's okay," Antoinette said. "Nobody's after me. The authorities think I'm dead."

"I have a little boy," Cathy said. "I can't afford to get in trouble."

"You won't. I'm done with the supervillain thing. I want a normal life, and I want it in the town where my family is. Can I come in?"

After another moment, Cathy let her into the cramped living room of her side of the duplex. A stale smell hung in the air, and a brown stain mottled the ceiling. Gunfire, or rather, the sound of it on the neighbors' TV, banged through the wall.

Antoinette frowned. "That's kind of loud for this late at night."

Cathy waved her to an armchair with a tear at one corner of the backrest. "The wall's thin, and you can't run complaining to people about every little thing."

"I suppose."

Cathy sat down on the couch. "Look, Nettie, I love you and I've missed you every single day. But you're also why I had to change my name and move across country just for a chance at a normal life. Before I even think about having anything more to do with you, I need to know: Why are you doing this, and why are you doing it *now?* How can I be sure you mean what you're saying?"

Antoinette felt hurt. "When did I ever lie to you?"

"When you were lying to yourself, too."

Antoinette sighed. "Okay. Maybe that's fair. So let me tell you about the fabulous life of a supercriminal. The police shoot at me. Heroes as strong as elephants beat me up. I work with people I can never trust stealing money I almost never spend on anything fun because I'm too busy running and hiding. If you were me, wouldn't you quit?"

"Yes, but I'm not you."

"I swear, I'm done with it."

Cathy studied her the way Dr. Umbra had. Then she smiled. "All right, then, sis. Welcome home."

*

The duplex didn't look any less shabby in the morning light. The noise from the neighbors' TV–now it was the giddy babble of a talk show–still leaked in from next door.

But if Antoinette's surroundings scarcely seemed like an improvement over the rattiest safe houses where Sweet Lady Q had gone to ground at one time or another, the company was. Paul, her nephew, was a skinny, towheaded kid in love with astronomy and astronautics. She was putting off telling him who she really was until she was sure he could keep the secret, so she couldn't say that she herself had flown in orbit and visited the moon. But she could still talk knowledgably about space travel, and the two of them hit it off.

His chattering enthusiasm brightened up the place while they crunched their way through a breakfast of store-brand corn flakes and Cathy hurried off to one of her three part-time jobs. Antoinette enjoyed it enough that, when he had to leave for school, she offered to walk him to the bus stop.

Paul almost seemed to flinch. "No. That's okay. Mom said you have stuff to do." He grabbed his backpack and scurried for the door.

Antoinette sighed. Maybe Paul wasn't as taken with his mother's "friend from college" as he'd seemed. Antoinette was okay for a stranger and a grownup, but he didn't want her around to cramp his style when he was with other kids.

Still, they'd bond. She was sure of it. She freshened up her coffee and fired up Cathy's elderly Toshiba PC to check the local job listings.

*

Antoinette had to ride her own bus, a city-transit one, to follow up on what little she'd found online. The bus rolled along at a leisurely pace and stopped every block or two to let someone on or off, the folding doors squeaking open and shut. Remembering the Porsches and Maseratis she'd raced for fun and the even faster vehicles bristling with exotic weaponry she'd driven to hijack armored cars and kidnap dignitaries from motorcades, she wondered how anyone endured this waste of time on a daily basis.

But the other passengers didn't look like they minded, and that was because they had good lives with families, homes, and peace. They didn't have to fight the Balance or Osprey over and over again or rot in jail for months at a stretch till they managed to break out. That was a *real* waste of a person's precious time.

As the bus lurched to yet another stop, she told herself she was lucky to be onboard.

*

The telephone buzzed. Everybody in the crowded waiting room looked up at the same time like Pavlov's dogs reacting to a bell.

The secretary with the narrow, wrinkled face and blood-red lipstick picked up the phone and listened for a moment. Then she called out to the people in the molded plastic chairs.

"I'm sorry. That's all the interviews for today."

The job seekers looked back like they didn't understand. But apparently they did, because they started rising stiffly and trudging out.

It was Antoinette who didn't understand. She pushed against the outgoing tide to reach the receptionist's desk. The woman gave her a tight-lipped flicker of a smile. "Can I help you?"

"'That's all the interviews for today.' What does that mean?"

"That Mr. Geraghty has filled all the openings."

"Without seeing everybody? I had an appointment. I made it online."

She had a solid résumé and references, too, far better than these low-level retail jobs should have required. She'd paid big money to Mr. Quill to create her fake identities because he always delivered a quality product.

"It's the bad economy," the receptionist said. "We get so many applicants. If Mr. Geraghty saw everybody, that would be all he ever did."

I was here on time, Antoinette thought, *and when you didn't call me, I waited another hour and a half.* Her power stirred, warming the core of her and tingling down her arms.

She took a breath, and the sensations faded.

*

Yelling shrilled down the block. A twinge of curiosity roused Antoinette from a dullness born less of fatigue (it took a lot to tire out a metabolism capable of generating hundreds of thousands of amps) than frustration.

After she'd gone to the places the Internet told her to try, she'd wandered around downtown looking for Help Wanted signs. She hadn't found many. Quite a few establishments had gone out of business, like the whole city had fallen victim to the drabness she'd already discovered in Cathy and Paul's duplex and its rundown neighborhood.

Finally, when the surviving offices, stores, and sandwich shops started shutting down for the day, she'd taken another creeping bus ride home.

Squinting against the late-afternoon sun shining in her eyes, she spotted running figures. Paul was in the lead, but just barely. The other boys were going to catch him in a few more seconds.

Her hands feeling like they were vibrating on the inside, she trotted forward. "Hey!" she shouted. "Hey!"

Startled, the other kids balked. That gave her time to reach her nephew. Panting, he looked at the ground, not meeting her gaze or anybody else's.

"What's going on?" she asked.

The biggest kid twisted his square, flushed face into an expression that fell just short of being a sneer. "We were just messing around playing tag. Tell her, Paulie."

"Yeah," Paul said. "Just playing."

One of the other boys snickered.

"Come on in the house," said Antoinette to Paul. "You need to do your homework." She stared at the other kids the way she'd learned to stare down even maniacs like Knyfe when the situation required it. "You kids should go home, too."

As they climbed up the concrete steps to the porch, and the television next door blared that somebody was a "ho," Paul mumbled, "That was nice, but I wish you hadn't done it. If they think I'm telling on them, that will just make it worse for me when there aren't any grownups around."

"That's why you didn't want me to walk you to the bus stop. They'd think you asked me along to protect you."

"Yeah."

"Why don't they like you?"

He shrugged. "I'm the new kid, and it's not a good school to go to if you're a science geek."

She hesitated, wondering if she should let Cathy handle this, then reflected that her sister wouldn't even be home from her various jobs until late.

"You know," she said, "you're right that you shouldn't rat. I mean, tattle. But running away won't help, either. You have to stand up to bullies."

Paul sighed. "People say that, but they'd just beat me up."

"Not necessarily. Let's go in the backyard."

As they passed through the house, she thought about how her instructors had gone about teaching her hand-to-hand combat. She'd decided to learn after a near-disastrous encounter with technology designed to dampen a superhuman's powers, and although she was no Scarlet Bride, she'd gotten pretty good.

"The first thing you have to know," she said, "is how to make a fist."

*

Hanging onto a metal pole, Antoinette looked around the crowded bus and recognized many of her fellow passengers. They caught the bus out of downtown at this same time every day, which meant *they* had jobs.

And God, wouldn't her old partners have laughed to hear that she envied them. Sweet Lady Q, who could walk into any bank in the world, toss some lightning around, and walk out five minutes later with all the money she could carry, was jealous of losers who had no choices in life but to kowtow to bosses like Mr. Geragthy's bitch of a receptionist and grind away at boring tasks day after day after day.

But no. That was the wrong way, the self-destructive criminal way, to look at it. She made herself focus on what she planned to teach Paul this afternoon, and that helped her relax.

*

Antoinette knelt down in the grass so Paul could easily strike at her face with the final move of the combination. "Whenever you're ready," she said.

He checked his stance, lifted his hands, and then hesitated.

"You won't hurt me," she said. "You'll stop the final attack short, and if you don't, I'll duck."

"Okay," said the boy, "but isn't this, like, *dirty* fighting?"

She snorted. "Are there four bullies and only one of you?"

"Yeah."

"Then do what I tell you."

*

Cathy waited until Paul was in bed to sort through her mail. Most of it was bills, some marked Overdue or Final Notice. She closed her eyes and massaged the bridge of her nose with her thumb and forefinger.

"You look unhappy," said Antoinette.

"I have a headache."

"Is there anything I can do to help?"

"You can get that job you're supposed to be looking for."

"I *am* looking."

Cathy sighed. "I know. I'm sorry. It's just that Jack doesn't pay his child support, the school system lays me off, I run up student loans getting my stupid degree in Medical Office Management, nobody will hire me to do that, either–"

"And then your long-lost troublemaking sister shows up on your porch like a stray dog."

Cathy winced. "I swear to God, I'm not complaining about that. I'm thrilled you're here. I just wish I could catch a break."

Antoinette smiled. "I'll let you in on a secret. You already have. I didn't tell you before because you acted so nervous about having me around at all, but I've still got some of the money I stole. I shouldn't transfer it for at a while, but as soon as it's safer–"

"I don't believe this!" Cathy exploded. "You swore you were done with all of that!"

"I am! I'll never, ever commit another crime. But we might as well use what I took already. You and Paul can have a better life."

"Or I can go to prison for harboring a fugitive, and he can go to foster care! You can have your...loot or your family, Nettie. You can't have both."

*

The stain on the living-room ceiling was just visible in the gloom. Antoinette lay on the couch and stared at it while, next door, an infomercial raved about the wonders of a "revolutionary weight-loss drink."

She needed the infomercial to shut up so she could fall asleep, put her sister's paranoid ingratitude in the past, and wake up liking her again. She wrapped a pillow around her ears, and, when that didn't keep out the noise, got up and padded out onto the porch in her borrowed pajamas and bare feet. She peeked in a window at the front room of the other half of the duplex.

No one was there. The neighbors had apparently left the set on when they went upstairs to bed. What kind of idiots would do that?

Idiots who didn't realize who was living beside them.

It was a mild night, cool but not cold, and the window was up. She poked her index finger through the screen and hurled a bright, pencil-thin twist of electricity at the television. The set crackled and then went silent and black. Smoke billowed out of the back.

She grinned.

*

"You're getting better," Antoinette said. "Your stance is balanced, and your blocks are working. But this time, give me all you've got. Hit and kick like you mean it."

His face sweaty, Paul said, "I guess I don't really mean it."

"Pretend I'm Roger." Roger was the beefy kid who'd claimed they were playing tag and was more or less the leader of the bullies. "What names does he call you? Chicken? Faggot? Is he right? Is that what you are, a little faggot? Faggot. Faggot. Come try and hit me, fag–"

Paul rushed her.

She blocked five attacks, then stepped back. "Stop. That was better, but–"

He came at her again.

She sidestepped and used a foot sweep to dump him onto the grass. "I said, stop."

Looking shocked at his own aggression, he goggled up at her. "I'm sorry!"

She smiled. "It's okay. That happens in training. People lose their cool. And you had the right instinct. In a real fight, *don't* stop, not until it's over."

*

Winston liked rock climbing and scuba diving and, judging from the way he kept talking about them, imagined that relating his self-proclaimed "adventures" was a good way to impress the opposite sex. Since it was at least more interesting than...whatever it was he'd said he did for a living, Antoinette sipped her Chablis and tried to look interested.

Sitting across from him in a dimly lit bar made a change from the duplex, anyway. The quiet next-door was a relief, but now she had Cathy watching her suspiciously, and just because she'd offered to share her money. How insane was that?

Things were mostly okay when Paul was awake, but tonight, after Cathy sent him to bed, the duplex started feeling particularly claustrophobic. Eventually, Antoinette went for a long, brooding walk, which led her here and to Winston.

She abruptly realized she'd stopped listening to him a while ago, and now he was looking at her expectantly. "Yes," she ventured.

He laughed. "You zoned out, didn't you?"

"Well...yeah. I'm sorry."

"No, I am. I know I go on and on sometimes. Maybe instead of talking, we should dance."

That was a little more fun, enough so that when he asked for her number, she gave it to him. But when he drove her home and kissed her good night, the touch of his lips didn't make her feel much of anything.

Well, everybody knew, the first time could be tentative and awkward. The next one would be better. As she stood on the porch and watched his taillights recede into the dark, she tried not to compare him to *real* adventurers like Nexxt, Orcan, or even Dr. Umbra.

*

The people standing around Antoinette jostled her whenever the bus sped up or slowed down. The vehicle was so crowded they couldn't help it.

It's a damn cattle car, she thought.

Selfish though it was, she couldn't help wishing some gentleman would offer her his seat. But nobody did.

Sweet Lady Q could have *scared* an ordinary person out of his seat. She could have emptied out the whole bus.

A teenager with blue streaks in her hair sniffed twice. "Weird," she said.

"What?" asked her friend.

"It smells like it's going to rain. But we're inside a bus, you know?"

Antoinette shoved past a fat man to snatch the bell cord.

As she watched the bus roll away, she took deep breaths and told herself to be proud. She'd made the right choice and kept her self-control. Then her cell phone rang.

*

Antoinette thrust all her cash into the cab driver's hand, turned, and then hesitated. With its landscaping and basketball court, Juvenile Detention didn't look particularly grim as such facilities went, and she doubted anyone in Reception was on the lookout for supercriminals in disguise. Still, the place was part of the great machine that was law enforcement, and she'd spent half her life trying to avoid getting caught in the gears.

But her sister had sounded frantic on the phone, so she took a breath and headed for the entrance.

Thanks to the metal detector, fluorescent lights shining down on speckled gray linoleum, and smell of disinfectant, the inside of the building was more institutional than the outside. Cathy was pacing back and forth. When she spotted Antoinette, she scurried to her and threw her arms around her.

As she hugged her back, Antoinette looked around and found a pair of chairs in a deserted corner of the waiting area. It might not matter in the present circumstances, but given a choice, she wasn't going to talk where the correctional officers behind the counter could overhear.

"All right," she said once they were sitting down. "Tell me what happened. I couldn't understand it all on the phone."

Cathy swiped at her eye. "I don't understand it all, either. The policemen at the school arrested Paul for assault."

"Simple assault?"

Cathy frowned like it was a weird question, but she answered. "Aggravated assault, and the people here said there could end up being other charges, too. Supposedly, Paul broke one boy's knee and gouged another in the eye. He could lose the sight in it. The doctors won't know until he's out of surgery."

Antoinette sighed. "Shit."

"It just can't be true! Paul would never, ever do anything like that."

"Not unless he didn't have a choice. The other kids were bullying him. It was self-defense."

Cathy stared. "How do *you* know?"

Antoinette hesitated. "He told me a while back."

"Why didn't *you* tell *me?*"

"You work fifty-five hours a week and come home exhausted. I thought this was something I could handle for you." And build a relationship with her nephew in the process.

"Handle it how?"

"By teaching him to take care of himself."

"Like the terrorists and murderers you work with take care of themselves?"

Antoinette glanced around to make absolutely sure no one was listening. "Please, keep your voice down. And okay, yes, I taught him some...rough techniques. They're easier to learn, and he needed moves that would give him a chance against multiple opponents. I didn't know it would turn out like this."

"Of course not, because you still have the same wonderful judgment you always did."

"Look, I'm sorry! But Paul will be all right. They can't convict him of anything when it was four kids beating up on one."

"You don't know that. We don't know who threw the first punch. Even if he does eventually get off, for now, he's stuck in here!"

Antoinette winced. Bad things had happened to her when she was in juvie, after she started getting into trouble but before her powers manifested.

"They'll hold a hearing," she said. "The judge will set bail."

"Even if he does, how am I supposed to pay it? Or hire a lawyer?"

"I told you, I have money stashed away."

"Right, because that's all we need, for the authorities to figure out Paul's bail came from his aunt the supervillain. If that doesn't convince them he's a budding sociopath, nothing will!"

The start of a headache drew Antoinette's forehead taut and tightened her jaw and neck. Then, however, the incipient pain melted into the shivering crawl of lightning along her nerves. The power concentrating itself in her hands, she smiled, and something in her expression made Cathy's eyes widen.

"Don't worry," said Antoinette. "You're right, this is my fault, but I can fix it."

"You don't mean you're going to break him out."

Antoinette snorted. "Of course not. If we can't even bail him out without screwing things up worse than they already are, what good would breaking him out do?"

"Then what?"

"You're going home so no one can connect you to what's about to happen. Then, tonight, Sweet Lady Q is going to go on a rampage through town." She grinned. "Who knows why? Sociopaths just do evil, crazy things."

Cathy shook her head. "Nettie, no."

"While I'm running amok, I'll blast this place to pieces. I'll trash the city jail and the police department, too. Afterwards, the authorities will have no choice but to release underage prisoners like Paul back to their families. They won't have anywhere else to put them. That will solve the immediate problem, anyway, and you can figure things out from there."

"No," Cathy repeated. "*Please,* forget what I said before. I was freaking out. This situation is bad, but not that bad. Somehow, we'll get Paul out without you throwing away the life you want."

"But I don't want it. I thought I did, but I was wrong. I mean, I want you and Paul. I love you, and I'll miss you every day. But normal life...I'm not saying I'm too good for it. It's probably too good for me. But I've gotten too *big* for it. All the boring parts, the disrespect, the little aggravations and disappointments...I don't know how to put up with them anymore."

Cathy studied her face. Then she said, "Promise me you won't hurt anybody."

"All right." Antoinette wondered if she'd finally succeed in keeping a promise. She hadn't done very well at it lately.

They hugged again, and then Cathy left. As the door swung shut, Antoinette marveled that it was possible to feel such profound loss and relief at the same time. She also wondered how to throw together some semblance of her costume.

www.ingramcontent.com/pod-product-compliance
Lightning Source LLC
Chambersburg PA
CBHW060746210726
48292CB00015B/2808